DARKE ACADEMY

LOST SPIRITS

DARKE ACADEMY
LOST SPIRITS

GABRIELLA POOLE

Hodder
Children's
Books

A division of Hachette Children's Books

ISBN 978 1 444 91018 6

Typeset in Berkeley by Avon DataSet Ltd,
Bidford on Avon, Warwickshire

Printed in the UK by CPI Group (UK) Ltd, Croydon, CR0 4YY

The paper and board used in this paperback by Hodder Children's Books
are natural recyclable products made from wood grown in
sustainable forests. The manufacturing processes conform to the
environmental regulations of the country of origin.

Hodder Children's Books
a division of Hachette Children's Books
338 Euston Road, London NW1 3BH
An Hachette Livre UK Company

PROLOGUE

The light was dim in the Chien Rouge, her favourite Brussels bar, but the glint off the bottles behind the bar was more than enough to make out the young man. Over the rim of her wine glass, she watched him appreciatively. Amber eyes, jet hair and golden skin; he didn't look entirely real. He looked like a very richly ornamented statue, except that she could see his fingers twitch, and she could make out the rise and fall of his breathing. And of course, there was the frequent lifting of that whisky tumbler. She eyed him closely as he took another drink.

Far too beautiful to look so sad. He needed a distraction. She allowed herself a little smirk of happy anticipation. Rising, she picked up her expensive bottle of wine and carried it to the bar.

She lifted the handsome man's backpack off the stool next to him and slid on to it, clinking her glass against

1

his. Startled, he glanced up, nervously snatching for the backpack and placing it on his lap before slumping back again.

'I'm sorry, do I . . . ?' he began.

'Know me? No.' She smiled. 'I hope you will, though.'

The man frowned. 'I'm not sure I—'

'Oh, forgive my forwardness. It's just that you look a little . . . lonely?' She ran a hand through her brown-blonde hair, letting it catch the light. 'I wanted to cheer you up.'

A light of interest kindled in his eyes, and she bit her lip as she smiled again.

'What makes you think I want company?'

'I'm not sure you do want it. You certainly *need* it. I hate to see someone so beautiful looking so unhappy.'

He laughed, a low reluctant chuckle. 'Very kind of you, but I'd rather be on my own, thanks.' He took another swig of his drink. 'Anyway, I'm bad news.'

She tutted. 'If you knew how often I'd heard *that*. Don't you worry, I can handle it. Let me buy you another one of those. It'd be my pleasure.'

He hesitated, and she knew she'd won. Catching the barman's eye, she gestured at his tumbler. It needed refilling.

Scooting her bar stool a little closer, she raised her

glass in a toast. 'Here's to forgetting your troubles.'

'I doubt that.' But he raised his refilled glass, and the corner of his mouth quirked in an attempt at a smile.

'I haven't seen you in here before.' She looked him up and down. 'I'd have remembered.'

'No. I . . . move around.' His gaze had suddenly grown very intent and searching.

Sensing a chance, she placed a hand on his arm. The muscles trembled a little; she could feel them. This was a good sign.

'Where are you from, then? You're new to Brussels? Or just new to the Chien Rouge?'

'That's a lot of questions.' He turned a little more to face her, and she definitely saw the intense glint of attraction in his eyes.

'Well, answer the first one first.' She laughed, tossed her hair again. 'Where are you from?'

He shrugged. 'Lots of places.'

'And where are you headed?'

'Anywhere but here.'

'You are terrible at answering questions!'

He leaned forward, reaching over to place his hand against her cheek, and she started slightly. Partly it was surprise – who was being forward now? – but partly it was the spark of desire that flickered across her skin at his touch. He looked young, but his eyes had that look of age and experience that made for an enticing combination. Leaning closer, she gazed into them. They were extraordinary eyes: full of emotion and life and passion. And something else, something she couldn't quite make out. A light, but a turbulent one . . .

Unable to resist, she closed the small distance between them and pressed her lips impulsively against his. For a moment he went completely still; then he was responding with a ferocity that almost shocked her. Desire raced through her body like a lick of flame, and she felt the strength drain from her muscles. His fingers raked through her hair, tightening on the back of her skull.

It was incredible. Unbelievable. Helpless in the grip of frantic lust, she even thought for a wild moment that she was going to pass out with the excitement of it all. And then she realised: something was wrong. Her consciousness was actually beginning to drain away.

Her eyes snapped open, panicked.

His were wide already, hungrily fixed on hers. Struggling now, she managed to push him away. The light in his eyes was beyond extraordinary now. They were almost – entirely – red—

She fell back, tearing her hair from his grasp, staggering from her bar stool and only just keeping on her feet. His hand snatched at her arm again, though whether to stop her falling or drag her back to him, she couldn't tell. Staring at him, she gripped the bar stool with both hands, holding it between them like a shield.

'I told you,' he snarled, breathing hard and fast. 'I'm bad news.'

Stiffening, mustering her dignity and getting her breath back, she curled her lip, trying to stop shaking. 'Y-you're drunk!'

'No kidding.' He shut his eyes, wobbling on his stool.

When he opened them again, they were normal; no longer that unnatural red, though perhaps a little bloodshot. She'd imagined the glowing. She must have.

'Get away,' he growled. 'Get away from me.'

'My pleasure,' she told him haughtily, though her voice still shook. 'You need help.' She glanced at the barman as she stalked away.

'I wouldn't give *him* any more,' she snapped, and slammed the door of the bar behind her as she hurried away.

You need help.

Oh God, that was truer than she knew. Flinging a few notes on to the bar, Ranjit seized his backpack and almost ran to the door. Outside, the Brussels rain stung his face and brought him to a halt. He took a breath and tried to orient himself, taking the opportunity to double-check yet again that the fastening on the backpack was secure, then hunched his shoulders and hurried on into the night.

He'd come *so* close to losing control. He'd tried really hard lately and so far it had worked, but she'd come on so strong, and his spirit was so hungry. And what's more, she'd been sweet, and gutsy, he couldn't help being reminded of—

No! Don't think about her . . .

He couldn't let it happen again. When he'd . . . Ranjit hesitated even thinking about it. When he had killed Jake in Istanbul . . . and come so close to killing Richard, he didn't know whether he'd betrayed his spirit, or his spirit had betrayed him. It didn't matter. It wasn't going to happen again. Regardless of the role the cursed Pendant had played in what he'd done, he had to have been responsible on some level. He'd blown it forever, he knew that. He would never see Cassie again, so the fact that he had no idea what the hell he was going to do now didn't seem to matter anyway. Oh, God, why had he thought the Pendant would be the key to him and Cassie being together? How could he have been so *stupid*?

Disgusted at himself, and filled with remorse, all Ranjit

felt he could do after the horror at Hagia Sophia was run. Cities had proved a good place to hide: bustling, crowded, anonymous. His spirit needed to feed, as it always did, but he could keep its hunger at bay with vagrants and drunks and lost tourists. With longing he remembered the easy days at the Darke Academy, feeding from his cooperative roommate Torvald.

He wouldn't let himself remember what else, who else, he'd left behind.

At the mouth of a dark and rain-soaked alleyway, Ranjit came to a halt. Something was in the air: a vague threat, an aura of harm. Slipping the backpack nervously from his shoulders, he clutched it tightly against his chest. Money be damned; but the thing in the backpack, the Urn that he'd stolen from Sir Alric Darke in his time of madness? That he must not lose.

That, and his self-control.

He wouldn't even harm a mugger. Let them take everything, so long as they left him his soul, and the Urn. All the same, his muscles were tense as his bleary gaze searched the darkness, and he could hear his heart thrashing.

And then he saw them. At first they were only vague shapes, and he realised he'd drunk more than he'd thought. And then they walked towards him.

NO! It couldn't be!

He was dreaming, surely. A nightmare through the warped haze of alcohol. Shock immobilised him for just a second, and then the fear kicked in, colder than the rain. They stalked forward, one to his right and one to his left, and he saw their pale hair glitter in the streetlights. That confirmed his worst fears, even before he belatedly, blurrily focused his mind, and recognised the dark spirits glowing in their chests.

Brigitte and Katerina Svensson. Renegade spirit-hosts, banished from the Few. But still alive. Clearly still very much alive – and deadly.

He snarled, but his first instinct was to grip the backpack tighter rather than lash out, and he wasn't ready when they lunged for him. Stumbling back, he tried to kick out at them, but in his desperation to hold on to the Urn, he lost his balance.

Dammit, he thought. You *are* drunk.

Katerina leaped, grabbing his head in a powerful underarm lock, dragging him backwards as Brigitte tore at the backpack and slammed a powerful punch into his midriff. Doubling over on the ground, Ranjit tried to curl himself protectively, but Katerina's grip on his neck was too strong, and Brigitte's blows were coming hard and fast.

His right foot caught Brigitte in a fierce blow to the chest, and she staggered back, but it was a lucky fluke. As he tried to follow it up by striking out at Katerina with one arm, Brigitte recovered fast and grabbed the backpack. He gave a single howl as he felt it ripped from his weakened grip.

He could fight them properly now, get it back. But as his view of the Few women reddened with his eyes, as the rage inside him began to boil, something inside caused Ranjit to freeze for a split second, and it wasn't his spirit.

What if he *did* kill them?

No. I won't kill again! Not even them. I can't give in to it—

But he knew he *must*—

Too late.

Brigitte and Katerina were raining kicks and blows on him now, claws raking at his eyes and skin. The world began to fade as blow after supernatural blow struck him. His skull hit the pavement hard, and the streetlights above him whirled and exploded in a dazzle of pain. Cruel hands gripped his arms and began to drag him away, scraping his skin against concrete and tarmac. His ears rang; there was a screaming in his head, but through it all he could hear their triumphant, disbelieving laughter, their cries of savage joy.

'We have him! He's ours! WE HAVE HIM!'

CHAPTER ONE

Cassie Bell stared out of the small oval window. Below her the land seemed endless, a yellow expanse dotted with scrubby trees and threaded with rivers and the ancient tracks of animal migration. Kenya, from this height, was wildly beautiful. Her mind buzzed with anticipation, and not just of a new term in a stunning new location. This was going to be the term when she turned everything around. *Everything*.

And yet, despite her determined positivity, Cassie's heart was hardly brimming with happiness.

'Are you OK?' she murmured to her best friend at her side.

Isabella Caruso only nodded, her eyes empty, and stared towards the cockpit. Cassie felt the familiar frisson of unease. Isabella hadn't so much as glanced out at the landscape since they'd taken off from Nairobi airport. Far from the bouncy, excitable Isabella of previous terms, she seemed glazed, a walking automaton.

'Hey, ladies,' Richard Halton-Jones bawled from the cockpit. The flying conditions were tricky, and he was clearly enjoying the challenge of the strong winds against the Cessna jet. 'Did I tell you about Yuri Tretschnikov and the Siberian gas heiress? Wait till you hear *this* . . .'

Cassie was glad of Richard's banter, even if he did have to yell his gossip over his shoulder above the noise of the plane. He must be used to this awkward form of conversation; after all, this was his very own small twin-engine plane. Presumably his parents had bought it to go with his string of polo ponies.

That, Cassie thought, was an unworthily bitchy thought from her. She didn't know where she'd have been without Richard last term, after the murders at the Darke Academy and all that had unravelled at the Hagia Sophia. And he'd made it more than clear that if she had to give up on Ranjit Singh, he would be there to catch her as she fell . . .

Part of her really wished she could love him that way too. How much easier it would be to find solace in Richard's secure embrace than to go on placing her faith in Ranjit? But even if she tried, she knew it would be a lie. Cassie knew that now better than ever. She'd made her decision last term, and she would stick with it: she would find Ranjit, get him back; it didn't matter what he'd done under the Pendant's influence, they could work it out together. She and Ranjit were meant to be together, and they would be.

And that was more than would ever happen for Isabella and her boyfriend Jake Johnson. He was gone now. Cassie shut her eyes, feeling a renewed stab of grief. She'd be strong for her friend, she owed her that much. Isabella had lost so much more than she had.

Opening her eyes again, Cassie placed a hand on Isabella's arm. 'Look,' she said softly. 'Did you hear Richard? We're above the Tsavo national park.'

'Are we?' Isabella turned obediently to look out, but listlessly.

'Not a lot of shopping down there, I'm afraid!' shouted Richard cheerfully. 'We'll try Malindi one day.'

'If you don't take us on a game drive on day one, we'll never speak to you again!' Cassie shouted back. 'I take it you have some kind of stretch-jeep with a cocktail bar and a chauffeur?'

'Are you *mocking* me, Scholarship Girl?'

'I certainly am.' Cassie nudged Isabella and gave her a wink, but Isabella didn't even attempt a laugh, and Cassie felt her mood sink again.

Even Isabella's usually glossy dark hair looked lifeless, and was pulled back in a rough ponytail. Cassie knew her friend had come back to the Darke Academy only after much persuasion and begging from her parents, and then only because she hadn't wanted to worry them any further by refusing. The Carusos had hoped – and Cassie still hoped – that a term in Kenya would begin some kind of a healing process in Isabella's soul. It wasn't looking good so far.

And yet Cassie was actively looking forward to the new term, despite her sense of guilt. Kenya seemed the ideal choice: wildness and space and open air, after three consecutive terms in cities. It would be good for all the students, she thought, and especially for the Few – Richard, Ayeesha, Cormac and the others – after the calamitous events in Istanbul. They all needed some space to regroup. She wouldn't have been surprised if Sir Alric Darke had made his choice on that basis. As far as she knew, the school's changing location each term was his decision alone, however much he had to answer to the Council of Elders for the actions of his students.

Cassie shivered, remembering her own confrontation with the terrifying Elders, two terms ago in New York. When she'd come so close to being sent to the Confine for life . . .

For the first time, Isabella seemed to notice what was going on around her, and this time she squeezed Cassie's arm.

'What about you, Cassie? Are you all right?' There was concern in her voice that only sharpened Cassie's sense of responsibility. *If it hadn't been for Ranjit, Jake would still be alive. If it hadn't been for Cassie, her insane boyfriend and his crazy plan for them to be together backfiring so spectacularly . . .*

'Don't worry about me, Isabella, for heaven's sake!' Cassie laughed lightly, shaking off the memory. After all, what had she just been thinking? A new location, a chance to breathe and think, plenty of time and space to plan. Council of Elders be damned – indeed, Sir Alric Darke be damned – she would track down Ranjit all by herself. She would find him, bring him back, help put things right. Or as right as they could be after all that had occurred.

'You've been so kind, Cassie. But last term—' Isabella took a breath. 'It was hard for you too.'

'I told you, don't worry about me,' Cassie whispered. 'I'll be fine. And so will you. We'll look after you.'

'I don't know, Cassie.' Isabella looked away again, clasping her hands tightly. 'I don't know if I will be fine . . .'

Her voice trailed off. Richard half-turned his head, raising his eyebrows at Cassie, and she returned his troubled look.

'Nearly there, ladies,' he called, clearly trying to keep his voice light.

The new subdued atmosphere at least gave her time to think a little more. She'd say nothing to the grief-stricken Isabella, who had good reason to be bitter, but she couldn't help the hope in her heart. Knowing what she wanted, knowing *who* she wanted, had given her a new strength of purpose. The horror of Istanbul could never be obliterated, but she knew as surely as she knew anything that she'd find Ranjit again, that they'd somehow be together again, and that everything would come right, even despite the Few spirit still eager to be entirely inhabited inside her.

She couldn't afford *not* to believe it.

Richard had been so supportive and understanding, in spite of his declaration of love last term; she wouldn't lose him as a friend. Hadn't he offered to fly her and Isabella to the coast in his private plane? She wasn't regretting the offer *quite* yet, despite the queasy way her stomach lurched with the aircraft. As for the spirit Estelle inside her, well, she wasn't quite so supportive . . .

I don't know what you expect, my dear!

The petulant voice made Cassie smile. So far Estelle was being non-confrontational to an extraordinary degree, probably for diplomatic reasons. Estelle knew what was in her head; the spirit always did. For all her wickedness and black sense of humour, Estelle knew how much Cassie loved Ranjit, knew of her determination that they'd one day be together.

And for her and Ranjit to be together, Estelle had to go.

I refuse to discuss this at present.

Cassie grimaced. So long as you're not just biding your time, old girl . . .

No response, and for now Cassie had to be happy with that. The whole thing wasn't going to be easy – as Ranjit's experiment with the Pendant had proved. Sighing quietly, she gazed out of the window again at the magnificent sprawl of the savannah below her.

'All right, ladies,' called Richard. 'Nearly there. I can see the landing strip now. I'm just descending. Tighten your seatb— Whoa!'

The little plane lurched and bucked, swaying wildly. Cassie grabbed her armrest as she was flung sideways, almost into Isabella's lap.

'Richard?' yelled Cassie.

He didn't answer for long moments, wrestling with the controls. At last he gasped, 'Turbulence! It's OK, I can—'

But he didn't finish; he was focused on the plane again. Cassie glanced at Isabella; the Argentinean girl was gripping her seat, jaw tight and skin pale. Cassie undid her seatbelt and managed to wriggle out, grabbing anything close for support, as she stumbled to the cockpit.

'Go back!' yelled Richard. 'It's fine.'

'No! Can't I help?'

'Not unless you can fly a bloody plane! Sit down!'

But the plane at that moment took a crazy plunge, and Cassie had to hang on to the pilot seat for dear life while Richard struggled to bring its nose back up.

'I wish you'd let me—'

'Cassie, go back!'

Thrown against the cabin bulkhead, Cassie thought wryly that she wouldn't be wearing her bikini for a while, not with all the bruises she was getting. Bracing herself against the control panel, she ducked to look out of the window, and instantly wished she hadn't. The land was racing towards them at a most unlikely angle.

'It's absolutely fine,' yelled Richard. 'I'll just— Ah, bugger!'

'What?'

'Control's stuck. Don't panic!'

Men! she thought grimly. 'That one there?'

'Obviously!' He was wrestling with it.

Shutting her eyes and instantly reopening them, she focused. The world around her turned red as she projected her spirit beyond herself and into the cockpit, coiling it round the lever. Richard let go with a yelp of surprise.

'Jeez!' Sweat sheened his face, but his expression changed as he saw what was happening. 'Whatever you're doing, keep doing it!' he shouted, grinning.

Cassie felt her jaw ache with the effort of concentration. And then, abruptly, the lever released and the plane gave a last buck-and-leap. But Richard had control back and the juddering Cessna was finally levelling. Easing towards the ground at a shallower angle, it no longer felt as if they were being shaken by a giant fist.

'We're there! You did it!' yelled Richard.

The landing might not have been the smoothest she'd ever experienced, but the plane thumped down and rumbled to a halt. It seemed to sigh with relief itself as red dust settled round its wheels. Cassie flung her arms round Richard and hugged him, and he returned the embrace with enthusiasm.

'Well done, Halton-Jones. That was a hell of a landing!'

'Well done both of us! You can fly with me any time, gorgeous.'

She laughed. They knew each other too well now for any awkwardness.

19

Together they turned to look at Isabella. Her face was still white, but her hands didn't tremble as she undid her seatbelt and pulled herself to her feet, ducking her head in the tiny cabin. Her lips were compressed in a firm line. Well, thought Cassie, she's been holding herself together since Jake died. It might be becoming second nature – but that worried Cassie . . .

'Yes, well done, guys,' Isabella said quietly. 'Though, Cassie, you're a reckless girl to do what you did. I was afraid for you.'

Isabella's smile was strained, and Cassie didn't think that was only down to nerves. What must go through her best friend's head now, when she saw Cassie's unusual Few power deployed? Cassie shook herself as Richard creaked the plane's door wide and the coastal heat struck them.

'Thank you for flying Bronco Airways, ladies.' He grinned, and flung out an arm towards the country beyond. 'Welcome to Mombasa!'

CHAPTER TWO

Not *quite* Mombasa, as it turned out; Cassie had been expecting the school to be located in the heart of the ancient coastal town, but the new Darke Academy was a few miles to the south. It felt strange to ride in the air-conditioned car that had been dispatched to collect them, and she rubbed her goose-pimpled arms even as she gazed out through thick glass at equatorial vegetation and turquoise seas. Wanting to feel the air and smell the atmosphere, she surreptitiously leaned a finger on the window control, and it slid down. Warm damp air rushed in.

Gratefully Cassie sucked in the hot scent of oleander and dust, even as Richard shook his head and leaned across her to wind up the window with an impish grin. Marat the porter-cum-general-factotum, who was driving, took no notice of any of them.

21

Cassie smacked playfully at Richard's arm, wrestling it away. 'Come on, Ricardo. Soak up the atmosphere!'

'I *will* be soaking,' he complained, tugging his damp shirt away from his skin. 'Ugh. Isabella, control this barbarian!'

Isabella seemed not to hear, just went on staring out of the opposite window at spiky plantations of sisal. Once again Cassie and Richard exchanged troubled glances, settling back in their seats.

'Not much further, I don't think, anyway,' he murmured. His face brightened as he leaned forward, pointing. 'Ah! Thank God. That's it!'

Cassie too leaned forward eagerly; she couldn't imagine that she'd ever lose the thrill of spotting the new Academy each term. The building was barely visible as they turned into a long driveway lined and overshadowed by flamboyant trees, but each moment it revealed more of itself. When Marat turned the car out of the trees into a wide circle in front of the house, Cassie gasped.

The other mansions and hotels they'd passed on the road from Mombasa had been white stuccoed Arab-style affairs, but this great house was built of warm stone and roofed with red tiles. Set back from the sea, its gables were draped in vines and bougainvillea. It looked quite old, but 'It was built in the 1930s,' said Richard casually.

'Sort of a holiday house, for a tea planter up near Nairobi.'

'*Holiday house*,' echoed Cassie sarcastically, taking in the size of it. It was a world away from that modern city, the skyscrapers and the sprawling, teeming slums of Kibera. 'I suppose the whole country was different back then, anyway.'

'Very different,' said Richard, 'but in some ways it's always the same. Bit like the Academy, really.'

Even Isabella mustered enough interest to lean forward and gaze up at the windows that glinted in sun and sea-light. 'It is very beautiful,' she murmured.

And the beauty meant nothing to poor Isabella, thought Cassie sadly, without Jake here to share it. Cassie felt another pang of grief for him too, and chasing after that came unwanted thoughts of Ranjit. He'd been insane, when he killed Jake – *insane*, and through no fault of his own. It had been the curse of the Pendant that led to that disaster, and he'd only hunted down the Pendant because he wanted to make everything right between him and Cassie. He'd done it for *her*. Didn't that make her guilty too, in a way? Didn't it make her *responsible*? Yet it really wasn't her fault, and it wasn't his. In the truest of senses, Ranjit had been out of his mind.

Not that that made any difference to Jake or his family. Or to Isabella.

Marat was silent as he unloaded their luggage, but that was nothing new for the surly porter, and it didn't bother Cassie – she was used to his hostility. It gave her time to drink in her new surroundings, to inhale the smell of the ocean and the scent of tropical flowers. She took Isabella's arm.

'Let's go and settle in,' she said to Isabella, with a wave at Richard, hoping he'd understand and wouldn't take offence. He didn't; he'd already spotted Perry Hutton's eager face among the hubbub of returning students and was strolling towards him with a fresh swagger in his step.

Inside the mansion the atmosphere was cool and colonial, all white linen and mahogany furniture and gently turning ceiling fans, but it was loud with the voices of students pretending not to be excited. Cassie smiled to herself as she steered Isabella through the throng.

Cormac and Ayeesha shouted out greetings, and Cassie waved and grinned in response, noting the warmth of their Few auras hovering around them, Ayeesha's a little stronger than her boyfriend's. But Cassie didn't stop to chat, assuming instead an air of urgent preoccupation as she kept her forward momentum going. She didn't think Isabella would welcome a social gathering just yet. Other friends, of course, had moved on, having graduated from the Academy – Vassily, India . . . Cassie wondered where their Few lives would take them now.

In the high-ceilinged, marble-tiled hall she smiled with recognition at the statues that surrounded them. She'd once thought it odd that Achilles and Hector and Clytemnestra and the rest had to come with the school wherever it went; now they seemed like reassuring old friends who'd always be there for her. Even her terrified namesake Cassandra, cringing before the killing-blow, felt welcoming more than alarming.

Checking the document in her hand, Cassie led Isabella up a flight of stairs lined with striking Samburu artworks. The school wasn't such a maze as it had been in Paris or Istanbul, but their room was at the end of a small private corridor; thoughtful of Sir Alric, Cassie realised with reluctant gratitude. Isabella wouldn't be constantly bumping into people as she came in and out. Checking the polished brass plate – yes, *Miss Isabella Caruso; Miss Cassandra Bell* – she pushed the door wide.

She took a breath, as she always did at first sight of her quarters at the Academy. The room was huge, full of air and light, its tall casement windows open to the sound of the Indian Ocean beyond the palms; Cassie could see turquoise water glinting between the fronds. The beds were beautiful mahogany four-posters, hung with filmy

25

mosquito nets, and the desks looked too elegant for her battered old laptop. A gecko scuttled behind a painting, drawing her eye; the stunning impressionistic landscape of an African plain dominated one wall, almost giving Cassie the illusion she could smell the red dust.

In fact, she could smell flowers; the pink oleanders just outside the window smelled of baby talc, she thought, stroking a petal. And what were those – gardenias? And hibiscus! Leaning out, she plucked a scarlet flower.

She turned to Isabella, smiling, and tucked it into her friend's hair. 'That's better.'

Isabella touched it with a fingertip. 'Cassie. It's amazing how you can cheer me up.'

Really? thought Cassie doubtfully. But she said, 'Not enough, not yet anyway. Aren't you hot and dusty after that drive? Marat doesn't exactly make the time fly.'

Isabella actually giggled a little, for the first time since Cassie had met her at Nairobi. 'I know. He's so door.'

'*Dour,*' she corrected her friend absent-mindedly. 'Wow, look at that ocean. I know you'll have packed a million bikinis, right? And all of them beautiful.'

'I have one or two . . .' admitted Isabella sheepishly.

'So.' Cassie grabbed her arm with a smile. 'Let's go and christen them.'

* * *

26

'Careful, Cassie,' called Isabella anxiously from behind her. 'You don't know these waters.'

Cassie was already at the edge of the reef, the coral rough under her toes as she poised ready to plunge forward into deeper water. Isabella had hung back a little, crouching to examine shells and probe in rock pools, but now she was watching Cassie with anxiety.

'I'll be fine. Don't you worry about me!' Cassie called.

'Yes,' tutted Isabella, 'but you never know. There could be sharks, or sea urchins, or—'

'If there are sharks,' laughed Cassie, 'then they'd better watch out for *me*.' She flung herself forward with a whoop of delight, letting the cool clear water close over her head before surfacing and shaking it off. Flopping into a lazy backstroke, she floated, blinking up at the sun, then squinted back towards the beach.

There were other students venturing down to the water now, clutching snorkels and tanning lotion, and she could see even the snottier members of the Few splashing and hooting like kids as they dived into the crystal-clear water in huge fans of spray.

Cassie splashed upright and pushed her wet hair out of her eyes. Isabella had come closer to the edge of the reef, as if to dive in, but she had paused and was looking back at the school building, with its stones warm and glowing in the afternoon sun. The light was so clear here, Cassie could make out every fern frond, every vine, the lines and dents in every stone of the Academy. Still, she couldn't see any reason for Isabella to look so distracted by it.

'Hey, c'mon in!' yelled Cassie to her roommate. 'The water's lovely, as they say!' She splashed a little towards Isabella, who glanced at her, startled, but then returned her gaze to the huge mansion.

'I'm just coming . . .'

Cassie trod water, watching her friend curiously. 'What's up?'

Isabella couldn't seem to take her eyes off the high windows on the east wing of the house. Cassie hadn't noticed that part of the building until now. There was a narrow wrought-iron balcony that couldn't be seen from land, and French windows that led on to it, with fine muslin curtains that drifted in the faint sea breeze.

Isabella shivered a little, then turned and lowered herself gently into the deeper water beyond the reef. She took a few strokes and soon she was treading water beside Cassie.

'What was it? Did you see something?' Cassie said.

'No.' Isabella shook her head a little too vigorously.

'Go on, tell me?'

'I thought I—' Isabella glanced back at the balcony, her

brow furrowed. 'No, maybe I didn't.'

'I didn't notice that wing when we arrived. We'll have to check it out,' suggested Cassie brightly. 'There could be a secret spa or something lurking up there! Never know what you'll find at the Darke Academy, do you?'

'Or who.'

'What do you mean?' Cassie blinked.

'Forget it.' Isabella swam a couple of languid strokes, but her eyes kept being drawn back to the balcony. 'It's those curtains. I thought . . . I thought I saw someone.'

Cassie insisted. 'Who? Go on!'

'I don't—' Isabella hesitated, but then set her jaw. 'I'm seeing things. It was nobody.'

'Isabella, you have the eyes of a hawk. A hawk with binoculars.' Even with her heightened Few senses, Cassie had always been impressed by her friend's attention to detail.

The Argentinean girl didn't smile. 'I'm sorry, Cassie.' She sighed. 'I thought it was Jake.'

Oh, God. Instantly regretting both her good-natured nagging and the mistimed joke, Cassie felt her scalp prickle with horror. She ducked her head under the water for a moment to get rid of the alarming frisson. 'Isabella . . .'

'I know, I know. There wasn't anyone there at all. It was the curtains. They made shadows. Look, I'm sorry.' In a small voice she added, 'I feel like I see Jake all the time. Like . . . like he's haunting me, or something. It's awful.'

'Of course you do. And of course it is.' Cassie touched Isabella's arm as they floated in the water, and searched her face anxiously. She couldn't help remembering the horror she'd seen in Jake's eyes, the very first day she'd met him, in Paris, when he'd mistaken her briefly for his dead sister. And now, with a terrible irony, Isabella was seeing Jake, her own dead boyfriend, in shadows. Once again Cassie felt sorrow and guilt overwhelm her.

'Come on.' Gently she tugged Isabella's hand. 'Let's swim.'

'Yes. You're right. I need to get a grip.' Isabella struck out into the waves.

Cassie followed her. 'Isabella, wait! That's not what I meant.'

'I know, Cassie,' she called over her shoulder. 'But I mean it, I really do. It's so stupid. I wish I could just snap out of it.'

'Don't be so hard on yourself.' Cassie swam on her side so she could watch Isabella. 'It hasn't been long at all, since—'

'I can't spend the whole term, the rest of my *life*, just missing him,' interrupted Isabella fiercely, avoiding Cassie's eyes. 'I can't. It's happened. I need to try and move on. I just don't know if I can.'

Truly, Cassie couldn't see any alternative either, but she was damned if she was going to sit back and let Isabella be relentlessly unhappy. 'Well, we'll be really busy this term,' she comforted her friend. 'There'll be loads of field trips. And . . . And remember what Richard said? There's actual *shopping* up in Malindi!'

Shopping? Oh God, Cassie. As soon as the words were out of her mouth, they felt stupid and inadequate, and she rushed to drown their echo in her own head. 'You *will* have a good term, Isabella. As good as possible, I'll make sure of it.'

'Oh, Cassie, you're sweet.' Isabella smiled at her at last, floating on to her back. 'But a *good* term? That is perhaps a bit too much to expect.' She gestured with an arm, splashing water. 'Look at this fabulous place, and I can't even be excited about it. The Academy used to have such magic for me. And now . . .' She rubbed her face; Cassie suspected it was more than seawater she was wiping away.

'Too many memories,' she suggested softly.

'Yes. Too many memories. I never realised how much of this place was Jake. For me, anyway.'

31

'Maybe you'll get the magic back, with a bit of time?'

'Maybe, Cassie. But I'll never get Jake back, will I?'

There was nothing Cassie could say to that. Hurriedly Isabella turned her face away, and swam in a rapid crawl back towards the reef.

CHAPTER THREE

'Hey, Cassie! Isabella!' Books in one arm, Ayeesha used the other to give them each a swift fierce hug. 'You were elusive over the weekend! I saw you on Saturday and then you disappeared!'

'We were kind of . . . exploring. We weren't trying to avoid you,' lied Cassie with a stiff smile. 'It's great to see you again, Ayeesha. And you, Cormac!' She submitted to a hug from Ayeesha's eternally upbeat Irish boyfriend, and then he turned to Isabella, embracing her more soberly.

'We're so sorry about Jake,' he murmured.

'Yes,' said Ayeesha, putting an arm around Isabella's shoulders.

She nodded, clearly incapable of answering, so Cassie quietly said, 'Thanks.'

But oh, please, let's not pursue the subject right now . . .

The corridors were thronged with students on the first day proper of term, but there was a sense of even more reluctance than usual to get stuck into classes. Too much snorkelling and sunbathing over the weekend, thought Cassie fondly, had made them all very unprepared for schoolwork. For herself, she was glad to be starting classes again; she and Isabella had behaved like recluses after that first swim, hanging out in their room: painting their nails, reading, talking. It had been a lovely quiet start to the term, but for Isabella's sake, it couldn't go on forever.

'You'll have to excuse me, Ayeesha,' said Cassie solemnly, pulling Isabella along by the hand. 'I need to handcuff Isabella to me so she doesn't try and escape Maths.'

Ayeesha laughed a little too brightly. 'What's new! Eh, Isabella?'

Isabella's lips twitched and she nodded, but she said nothing, not even to moan briefly about the horrors of algebra. She eased herself away from them and preceded Cassie into Herr Stolz's classroom. Ayeesha and Cassie exchanged apprehensive glances, and Cassie shrugged.

'She'll be OK.'

'Oh, I hope so.' Ayeesha squeezed her arm anxiously, and hurried after Isabella into the classroom.

Herr Stolz's face brightened as he greeted Cassie, but for once she couldn't bring herself to act the star pupil. Throughout his lesson she was distracted, avoiding his pointed looks when he asked for answers. Even the nudges and giggles from the nastier Few, when Stolz ticked her off in hurt tones, couldn't make her concentrate on the value of y.

It didn't help that Estelle was making bitchy remarks in her head about her classmates, some of which made Cassie want to laugh out loud in spite of herself. She knew what Estelle was up to, but she couldn't help sort of enjoying her company when she was in this mood. The old spirit, split by Cassie's interrupted initiation into the Few, had never been backward about offering her opinions, whether Cassie wanted them or not, but she was sticking firmly to gossip, never deigning to mention Cassie's plans . . .

Yet she knew Estelle must be angry about her hopes to be free of the Few spirit – terrified, even. Cassie knew about Estelle's hatred for the half-joined nature of their union; she knew that such a division was horrific and unnatural for a Few spirit, and that it had never happened before. For Cassie to threaten her with total expulsion to that void must be the worst possible prospect for the wicked old bat.

And yet, Cassie couldn't help but feel oddly fond of her . . .

Still, these last few days with Isabella had only strengthened her determination to cast Estelle out. Perhaps she'd been in two minds about her decision at one point – quite literally in two minds, she thought with a rueful smile – but not any more. Isabella's misery was a sharp reminder of what Few membership could do to other human beings. Sure, there were good things about belonging to the Few – strength, beauty, contacts and influence were hardly to be sniffed at – and she liked some of her fellow Few enormously. But when she thought of what the Few had done to Jake – to his whole family – she knew it wasn't worth it. None of it was.

Above all, there was Ranjit. Ranjit and she could never be together while Estelle's spirit was in her; Sir Alric Darke had made that abundantly clear, and events had proved him right. Their spirits were incompatible, he said; it would be disastrous to bring them together.

But they *would* be together, of that she was absolutely certain. And if she was to be with Ranjit Singh, the spirit she still called Estelle Azzedine had to go . . .

Cassie shut her eyes, still remorseful, just as Herr Stolz's knuckles rapped the desk beside her, and she jolted. Someone at the back sniggered: someone Few, of course.

No one else would dare.

'Cassie Bell, what is wrong with you today? I've asked you three times to address this equation. You need not tell me you can't do it.'

'I'm sorry, Herr Stolz.' She gave him a guilty sidelong glance. His expression was more hurt than cross; how could his favourite student let him down like this? There was hope in his eyes too: she could solve the maths problem, and he knew she could . . .

Desperately reorganising her brain, she focused on the equation on the whiteboard.

Estelle, and Cassie's issues, would just have to wait.

As the evening settled and the tide was going out, Cassie stood on the exposed coral of the reef, staring up at the school. Against the indigo sky the beautiful building reared, an impressive silhouette, its open windows glowing with golden light. She could see the shadows of her fellow students moving around inside; even at this distance she could hear their laughter, their voices raised in happy conversation with friends they hadn't seen for the whole long summer.

She was supposed to be meeting up with Richard at

dinner, but she knew he'd be late as usual. Isabella had refused to come down to the dining room, probably unable to face the cheerful ribbing and gossip that were always so rife on the first night – or more likely she was anticipating the glances of pity and the not-quite-inaudible whispers.

To be honest, Cassie thought, she didn't much fancy being sociable herself, but it would be nice to chat to Richard without Isabella present. At least he'd take her concerns seriously; he might even have some suggestions for cheering the girl up. For such a joker, scoundrel and flirt, Richard was surprisingly good in a crisis.

Cassie glanced at her watch. He might have primped himself enough by now and be on his way to the dining room, she thought with an affectionate roll of her eyes. He'd want to look even more staggeringly attractive than usual for the new first years as well as for his returning friends and enemies, but surely even Richard couldn't take all night to get ready.

Attractive he certainly was, as well as a loyal and funny friend. Cassie was already looking forward to seeing him. Again she thought how different it could have been, if it weren't for the gigantic, undeniable complication of the fact that she was in love with Ranjit. Oh, if only life was simpler . . .

Time to go in, then. But as she glanced up again at the Academy's magnificent facade, she saw something that made her pause.

That balcony again. It was above what she'd worked out must be Sir Alric's office. She thought she had seen the filmy curtains move, but that alone was strange, since there was no breeze tonight, only the soft rush and whisper of a calm sea. If those curtains were stirring, it was because something had disturbed them. And Isabella had seen that shadow too.

Cassie narrowed her eyes. Was it the silhouette of a man, or just the night playing tricks?

It moved again. It was a person, she was almost certain of it. Someone who didn't want to be seen . . .

Absolutely motionless, Cassie stared up. Her heart leaped, and if her throat hadn't choked with crazy hope, she'd have shouted the name out loud.

RANJIT?

Don't be stupid, Cassie! Could she have imagined it? At this distance? No, she was Few. Not only was her eyesight better than a cat's, she knew what a stare *felt* like. And this one was intense. Clenching her fists tightly, she blinked, peering desperately, trying to catch a clear sight of . . . of what? This was crazy. Wishful thinking: Isabella was seeing Jake in the shadows, and now she was seeing Ranjit. The only difference was, for her – as least as far as she knew – there *was* even the remotest possibility it really could be her missing boyfriend. There was no chance of it being Jake, of course.

'Where *are* you, Ranjit?' she whispered out loud, tears threatening her sight. She swallowed hard and shook her head against the sound of her own voice, eerie against the murmur of the ocean, and the movement seemed to bring her to her senses. When she looked again, the curtains were still. It could have been anyone, she reasoned. Couldn't someone at the Darke Academy enjoy the view of the ocean without her gaping back at them like a love-struck fantasist? Bloody hell, Cassie. Get it together.

Cassie was quite sure now that she'd be late meeting Richard. He'd be mock-offended, but she knew she'd be forgiven. She hurried towards the building, knowing he'd be the one to help with forgetting her troubles. How could it have been Ranjit, anyway? The boy she loved was on the run, a murderer, hunted by the Few. He was hardly going to be hanging around the Darke Academy with a gin and tonic and a bowl of peanuts, just waiting for her to notice.

And besides . . . She *knew* what Ranjit's eyes felt like. She knew their burning, piercing power, and the way they cut straight into her soul; she knew the simultaneous chill and heat they sent through her bloodstream.

She knew what it felt like to have his eyes on her. That wasn't it.

CHAPTER FOUR

The elegant colonnaded dining room was open on two sides to the night air. Inside, chandeliers glittered, but where the room extended into the garden, it was flames from torches that sparkled off the silver and crystal on the tables. Cassie paused in the darkness beyond the torches, scanning the room in search of Richard; she spotted him quickly, leaning over a table of newly initiated Few girls and making them laugh flirtatiously. Clearly, with one of the weaker spirits amongst the Few, he was still playing his old game of making himself indispensable to everyone.

Cassie felt a surge of deep affection for her complex, unfathomable friend. She'd long since forgiven Richard for her unwilling initiation into the Few; and even if she couldn't ever feel for him what she felt for Ranjit – that violent, fierce, undeniable longing in her soul – what she did feel for Richard was pretty close to love.

Spotting Cassie, he raised a hand. Grinning, she sidled between tables and dodged students till she was at his side, exchanging a lingering kiss on the cheek rather than the air-kisses he bestowed on most of his acquaintances.

'Cassandra Bell, where have you been?' He raised a rakish eyebrow. 'I don't care if you're peckish. Hunting the wildlife for food is strictly forbidden.'

She laughed. 'Well, rhinos are a lot like chicken, you know.'

'I'm sure they would be, if there were any on the beach. I can see I'll have to take your education in hand *again*. Let's go on a game drive at the weekend. Tsavo. No, Shimba Hills. Let's go over here, there's a free table, minus any *objectionable* people.' This was said in a loud enough voice to earn him glowers from the tables he'd passed and rejected. People were still gossiping about what had happened last term. 'Sit down, Cassie. What do you want to eat, really?' He leaned closer. 'And let's choose quickly – I've got to tell you what I heard today about Marcia Gilbert. I'll give you three guesses, and you still haven't got a hope in hell. And anyway, you need to tell me about what you've been up to, and how Isabella's been. Come on, no clamming up, Ms Bell . . .'

'Clamming up?' she laughed. 'I haven't had a chance

to get a word in edgeways.'

She was more than happy to be swept along by Richard's enthusiasm, though. It saved her from having to acknowledge the hostile glances of Sara, Saski and the rest.

'So what are we going to do about Isabella?' Richard murmured eventually, in a quieter voice.

Cassie stroked the white linen tablecloth obsessively. 'I don't know. I'm not sure there's anything we can do. She's grieving.'

'Well, of course she is, even for yobbish old Jake.' He smiled sadly, taking the sting out of his words. 'Heck, Cassie, even I miss him. But I'm still worried. It's an important year and I . . . I just really don't want her to leave.' He sat back and spread his hands helplessly.

Cassie started. 'You don't seriously think she would?'

'No, but . . . Oh, listen, we'll make her better. You and me. That's what friends are for, right?'

'Right. But no flirting, Halton-Jones. She isn't ready.'

'Would I? You wound me,' he said sulkily. He paused for a moment and his mouth twitched at the corners. 'And you haven't even *asked* me about Marcia Gilbert and her father's intern.'

Cassie burst out laughing, drawing glares from Sara's table once more. Nobody could stay too gloomy around

Richard for long. There was definitely hope for Isabella with him on their side.

'Go on, then, you incorrigible rogue. Before you explode.'

Cassie declined Richard's offer to see her back to her room. He was her closest friend next to Isabella, and she loved hanging out with him, and she was certain he understood her feelings perfectly; but still, there was no point leading him on, or risking another impulsive kiss. He was irritatingly attractive, after all.

But Richard didn't deserve to be second-best to anyone.

Dinner had been delicious, as it always was, but she was uneasily aware of the *other* hunger sharp inside her, unsated by Mombasa oysters and fresh marlin and mango sorbet. Cassie had finally arrived at the moment she'd dreaded since she stepped on to the plane for Nairobi.

Patrick Malone, her friend and guardian at the care home, had helped her while she was back at Cranlake Crescent for the summer, by allowing her to feed from him in strictly controlled amounts. He knew all too well about the needs of the Few, having been a scholarship student at the Academy years ago himself. It had worked well, a perfect stopgap, but Patrick wasn't here now, of course. She was going to have to approach Isabella about it again – and there was nothing she was going to hate more.

Dawdling through the hall, reluctant to hurry back to their room no matter how the hunger grew and gnawed, she stopped to touch the Cassandra statue for luck. Stroking the white marble arm, extended in desperate, useless supplication, Cassie found herself sorrier than ever for the poor frozen prophetess, forever on the point of death by Clytemnestra's blade. When she gazed into the blank but terrified eyes of the marble figure, a shiver of pity went through her.

Oh for Zeus's sake, Cassie, it's only a statue! she scolded herself. Stop overreacting!

She was stepping reluctantly away from her namesake when she saw a shadow move out of the corner of her eye. Cassie went still, focusing on the darkness in the passageway that led to the library, then relaxed just a little.

Ah. It was no surprise to see who was lurking: the unmistakable, squat figure of Marat.

All the same, Cassie shivered. The porter still gave her the creeps, and not just because of his surliness. His hostility was palpable, and she knew he'd never forgiven her for the expulsion of Katerina after events in Paris. The little man was oddly fond of that evil Svensson clan. He gave Cassie a glance, but didn't smile or speak.

His very presence made her quicken her steps and hurry upstairs and along the corridor to her room. As she went inside, she found Isabella sitting almost where she had left her, on her bed, staring out at the night. A book was open on her lap, but she clearly hadn't been reading it. When she heard Cassie close the door, she attempted a smile.

'Cassie. How was dinner?'

'Good,' ventured Cassie lamely. She was uncomfortably aware that she was hovering.

Isabella eyed her. 'But not quite enough?'

Silence fell between them. Cassie looked down and began to pick at a fingernail, but that seemed cowardly and disrespectful. She raised her eyes to meet Isabella's.

'No.'

Swinging her legs over the edge of the bed, Isabella slowly unfastened her cuffs and slipped her sleeves up her bare tanned arms. She flexed her fingers together and then rested them on her knees, nodding slowly at Cassie.

'You'd better feed, then.'

Cassie's throat tightened, and an ache throbbed in her temple. She wanted to say *No, I won't. I wouldn't do that to you. Not after all you've been through. I'll think of something else. Anything.*

Instead she said, 'I'm really sorry. Yes, please, if I could. Isabella, I—'

'Don't. Don't say any more. It's got to be done. It's OK.'

Isabella avoided Cassie's sorrowful gaze and got to her feet. Swallowing hard, Cassie took hold of her wrists. They felt so fragile in her grip, the skin so delicate. She wished very much that Isabella would look at her and smile a little, but she couldn't ask that on top of everything else. Instead, Cassie simply tightened her hold, and focused on the life-force.

Nothing happened, and Cassie thought for a horrible moment that she wouldn't be able to feed after all, that she'd somehow lost the connection with her roommate. Then the life-force of Isabella began to flow, with a jolt that made Cassie's eyes snap open.

Isabella's were closed. A muscle twitched below her eye, and her throat jerked, but she gave no other reaction as the energy flowed out of her and into Cassie. Cassie stared at the veins in her friend's wrists, purple and prominent now against skin that was suddenly pale.

It wasn't at all like feeding from the old Isabella. The energy flowing sluggishly into her was like that of a stranger. There was no fizz, no sparkle, no effervescing life. Just a dark, reluctant sadness. She tasted . . . bitter, thought Cassie. Isabella was all bitterness and misery and sorrow. Even through the feeding process, Cassie could feel her heart ache for her friend.

As soon as the spirit inside her was satisfied, Cassie abruptly let go of Isabella's wrists, as if they burned. Taking a step back, she gazed at her friend, willing Isabella to open her eyes, to reassure her she was OK.

Then she saw it: a single tear trickling from beneath Isabella's long lashes down her pale cheek. Hurriedly, as if only just realising it was there, Isabella brushed it away and smiled – but the smile didn't reach her warm brown eyes.

'There, Cassie. That wasn't that hard.'

Cassie backed off, filled to bursting with Isabella's unhappiness as well as her own. It was almost unbearable, but she didn't have the right to cry over it, not in front of her friend.

'I'm sorry,' she whispered. 'I'm so sorry, Isabella.'

She turned, and ran from the room.

That was it. She couldn't do this any more.

Cassie couldn't go back to the room till she was certain Isabella was asleep, and she was desperate not to run into any of her fellow students: not even Richard. She strode along the beach until the lights of the Academy had almost vanished behind her, then slumped down in the sand and finally allowed herself to cry for five minutes.

Five minutes, she thought fiercely, gasping out a single sob. That's all. And then I'll start to do something about this. She rubbed her eyes with her sleeve, then the palm of her hand.

Isabella had lost the love of her life to the Few and their hideous twisted history. And Jake and his parents, before that, had lost Jessica. Cassie herself, despite her Few status and the protection it was meant to offer, had lost Ranjit to them. The Few had taken too much from all of them – were still taking it – and yet Isabella was still allowing Cassie to feed on her, to drain her of life-force. Despite all that had happened, all that Isabella had lost, she was spending her school career feeding a Few spirit, and she was doing it consciously and willingly.

It was too much. It was too much to ask of a girl who'd never shown her anything but friendship and trust and loyalty. It had to stop. Cassie gritted her teeth and wiped away her last tear. This was never something she had asked for, never something she'd wanted. She'd been tricked into becoming one of the Few, or the half-breed she ended up being with her broken induction ceremony. None of this should ever have happened.

There were two people who mattered more to her than anyone in the world: Isabella and Ranjit. They mattered more than her Few status, more than the spirit Estelle herself. By losing her Few status she would be able to have *both* of them back in her life, properly, with no demands and no guilt. How could she ever have hesitated? She had to sever herself from Estelle, whatever the cost.

Sir Alric Darke be damned. He had known all along that spirits could be split from their hosts. He'd kept it from her, the bastard; well, now he owed her big time, and she was going to collect. Finally, and conclusively.

The artefacts in his office: the ones that had caused such grief and strife? Well, the Pendant could draw a spirit out, and the Knife could sever the connection between spirit and host. Sir Alric possessed both of them; it was time for him to give them to Cassie. That wasn't in doubt.

Now all she had to do was ask him.

Well. Nobody had said it would be easy.

CHAPTER FIVE

Striding into the corridor outside the head of the Darke Academy's office, Cassie didn't even need to take a breath. She had never been so certain of anything in her life; she needed no courage – after all, she had only Sir Alric Darke to fight, not herself.

My mind's made up, she thought. I'm not sure I ever knew what that really meant before.

The anteroom to Darke's office was far less forbidding than the one in Paris, or even the one in Istanbul. Most of the windows were flung wide, so that Cassie could hear the gentle rustle of palms and smell the gardenia-scent that drifted into the room. Shifting sunlight dappled the colourful rugs, and she saw the shadow of a hummingbird dart across the floor; somewhere outside, a monkey screeched. The elaborately carved Maasai masks hanging on the wall behind Darke's desk should have been intimidating; but in the mood Cassie was in, they only seemed to encourage her. They couldn't look any fiercer than she felt.

The only blot on the interior landscape was Marat, who was kneeling at the open office door with a box of tools beside him. He didn't spare her a glance, but went on sulkily unscrewing the lock plate on the door. Cassie frowned a little, confused, then glanced up.

'Cassie Bell. Good to see you back.'

Sir Alric Darke: as imposing as ever, his mouth a severe line, his granite eyes frighteningly piercing. She would never conquer the twist of awe and slight fear in her gut at the sight of him, but it didn't matter any more. It was a feeling, that was all. She had more important ones to deal with.

Cassie took his proffered hand, knowing that despite his stern formality there were layers of relief beneath his greeting. He couldn't afford to have her going rogue, not after all that had happened.

'Good to be back, Sir Alric.' Despite everything, that was true. 'What happened to the door?'

'An attempted break-in last night,' he said, nodding towards the door. 'Nothing serious.'

Her eyes widened as she looked back at Marat and the toolbox. 'Nothing serious? A *break-in*?'

'Whoever it was failed,' Sir Alric said sternly.

Strange and unsettling how Cassie's mind went straight to Jake and his old habit of sneaking round the school after dark. But Jake was gone; and who else would do this? None of the students would dare. At least, none she could think of – not since Katerina's expulsion, and Jake's death.

'But who would—'

Sir Alric interrupted. 'Who knows? All that matters is that they didn't have the chance to do serious damage. It was a clumsy attempt. Marat and I both heard the commotion. Marat got here even faster than I did, but whoever it was had already got away – they must have been interrupted when they heard us coming.'

Cassie shuddered inwardly at the thought of anyone being caught in a crime by the strange, menacing Marat. 'That's all right, then.'

'It was a silly dare, I expect.' Sir Alric made a dismissive gesture. 'At the start of term I always expect some foolishness.'

Why didn't she believe him? Still, in front of the truculent Marat, she would take it no further. As Sir Alric gestured for her to enter his office, she followed, ignoring the sensation that Marat's eyes were boring into her turned back. What was going on inside that ugly bullet-head of his? Did he suspect *her* of doing this? It wasn't as if she hadn't been guilty before.

Just not this time.

Inside Darke's sanctum, little had changed. Little ever did, wherever the school went. The shelves were lined with the same books; the ornaments on the desk were familiar; even the atmosphere had the same taste of calm but intimidating authority.

Something was missing, of course. Its absence sent a horrible shiver down her spine: the Urn. Last time she'd seen it in his Istanbul office, set on a shelf as casually as if it was a mere ornament, Cassie hadn't known what it was, or what it could do. Now there was empty space where it should have stood; and to Cassie that gap seemed like a dreadful, menacing void. She knew now, of course, that it was one of the trio of powerful Few artefacts. And worse still was the sickening knowledge that the Urn had been in Ranjit's backpack when he fled from them all – and from himself – at the Hagia Sophia.

'I'd like a private word with Miss Bell,' Darke told Marat. 'Please leave us for a moment?'

Again Marat didn't speak; he simply gave a curt nod and got to his feet, picking up his tools and withdrawing from the anteroom.

The headmaster closed the office door firmly, but he

didn't sit down at his desk. Instead he nodded to a more comfortable chair beside the small table. Cassie recognised it as the one where she had shared tea with Estelle Azzedine, the former host of that troublesome spirit of hers, the woman whose name it had taken on. That was before the old woman had chosen Cassie as the new host, before she became Few. It felt like a century ago.

As she sat down hesitantly, Darke took a chair opposite her.

'Not many changes at the Academy, Cassie, are there?'

'There never are,' she murmured, glancing at her surroundings.

'And yet so much is different.'

'You read my mind.' Cassie blew out a breath, looking around. 'Hey, are those the Tears?' She pointed at an elaborately carved box on Sir Alric's desk, rather surprised that he'd left the cask of precious vials of healing Few liquid exposed.

'Yes. I brought them out to check on them after the break-in, naturally.' He went over and picked them up, locking them back in his safe, then sat back down in his chair and steepled his fingers under his chin. 'Not that there's much left of them. The Tears of the Few are sadly depleted these days.'

'It was worth it to save Richard.'

'Indeed.' He gave her a dark smile. 'I only use them in direst need, as you know.'

'Yes, it's partly my fault they're nearly gone as well, I suppose,' said Cassie crisply. Sir Alric had had to feed her with them at the start of her second term, when she'd still been fighting the notion of draining Isabella's life-force. Well, using up the Tears was something she *wasn't* going to feel guilty about. 'So you think whoever broke in was after them? Or maybe they were after the artefacts?'

Sir Alric blinked, but otherwise his face didn't flicker. 'I told you, it was more than likely a post-holiday prank. Why would anyone wish to steal these relics? They have no intrinsic value. At least, not to young people as wealthy as Academy students.'

'Except for the scholarship ones,' she put in acidly. She was so tired of the man's games. 'Sir Alric, just be straight with me. I know what the artefacts can do, and so do you. Why didn't you tell me sooner, before things went so wrong, with Ranjit and—'

'Why would I be *obliged* to tell you anything?' Sir Alric interjected sharply. He flexed his fingers and leaned forward, but Cassie didn't let her eyes drop from his.

'You had led me to believe that what they do wasn't possible.'

57

In silence they stared at one another. Cassie sat quite still, her jaw clenched. She could wait him out; let him be the one to break and explain himself. For once she felt not the least overawed by him. She could hold his gaze all day if she had to.

She didn't. Sir Alric finally cleared his throat and sat back.

'Fine. Indulge me, Cassie.' He no longer quite met her eyes. 'What is it that the artefacts do?'

'Shall I quote?' Anger sparked in her chest. '*Only this Knife may break the bond. The Pendant may be used to draw the Spirit from its Host. The Urn may contain and preserve a Spirit indefinitely.*'

Sir Alric closed his eyes and sighed.

'So,' she went on silkily, 'all that stuff about the ritual being irreversible was a lie, wasn't it? There was always a way to help me. You just didn't want to use it.'

'I'm sorry, Cassie.' He spread his hands. 'But it's true. I didn't want you to use the artefacts, and I still don't. Besides, at the time I wasn't in possession of all three, and now, thanks to Ranjit, I'm still not. So how are we any further forward?'

Cassie found she was breathing hard through her nose, determined to keep control. There would be no lashing out; not this time, because she had the upper hand. Sir

Alric wouldn't provoke her into losing her temper, and with it the argument. Pressing her lips together, Cassie gave him a tight smile.

'I have a proposition for you, Sir Alric.'

'Ah. You do?'

'Yes. But first, you're going to need to explain something to me.'

He laughed out loud. 'Cassie, I should have known when I saw you at my office door that I was in trouble. You had that look in your eye. What is it I have to explain? You seem to know such a tremendous amount already.'

She ignored his slightly waspish tone. 'I know how *I* found out about the artefacts. I want to know how *you* did. Is it common knowledge in the Council of Elders or something?'

'Yes and no.' He stood up, placed his hands on his desk with his back to her and gazed at the palms beyond the window. 'I lived in ignorance for quite a while myself.'

Clearly it pained him to make such an admission, she was glad to notice. 'Then you know what it feels like.' Cassie sat back and folded her arms.

He rubbed his forehead, clearly a little irritated. 'All right. I discovered the second half of the Few manuscript from which you so *accurately* just quoted some years ago. You know, of course, it was deliberately split into two halves by the ancient Elders?'

'Yes. That much I gathered.'

'I took it to the Council. We agonised over its rediscovery, we argued amongst ourselves, but we debated too long. We were too afraid of what the artefacts might do if they were discovered. Too willing to hope that if they remained unsought, they would remain unfound. Let sleeping demons lie, in other words.' He blew out a sigh. 'Probably our biggest mistake. Looking back, we were extremely short-sighted, and the rest of the Council regret that as much as I do.'

'Well, the first half of the manuscript told of exactly where the Knife and Urn could be found . . .'

Sir Alric shook his head. 'By the time I found the first half, it was too late anyway, the damage was done. Earlier, with the second half, we were all too afraid, and paralysed by indecision. We gambled that if we kept the existence of the manuscript and the artefacts to ourselves, the secrets would remain hidden. Perhaps we were too arrogant.'

Cassie rolled her eyes. 'You don't say.'

His wry half-smile told her he accepted that rebuke. 'Or, more accurately, we were too trusting. We – I – misjudged Brigitte Svensson, and underestimated her propensity for evil. A few months later I heard she was hunting for the artefacts, hoping to secure them and keep them safe; she'd used her Council influence to access and decode the half-manuscript. That news set my alarm bells ringing. I didn't know why, and I didn't know how long she'd been searching, but it suddenly seemed tremendously important to get to them first. I started to do the research I should have done before – to search for the second half of the manuscript, and through it to locate the Knife and the Urn.'

'But you didn't find them, did you?'

'Not all of them. I didn't discover the location of the Knife and the Pendant for many years, but by a stroke of luck as much as hard graft, I worked out where the Urn was. It seemed as if the Fates favoured me, because the Academy was moving to Mexico City the following term – and I hadn't even planned that, believe it or not. So I decided to wait. I had no reason to believe Brigitte had found out what I had, and it seemed sensible to arouse no suspicion. It was sensible, but it was next to impossible.'

Cassie could imagine that. If it had been her, she was pretty sure she couldn't have waited so long once she knew where the Urn was.

'I arranged a research sabbatical for myself early in the

61

new term. I knew I'd need an assistant, so as soon as everyone had settled in, I offered to take a particularly gifted Few student with me on the trip.'

'Erik Ragnarsson,' said Cassie flatly.

He raised his eyebrows, surprised, then nodded. 'But of course. His roommate was Patrick Malone, your guardian. So you know what happened?'

'The basics.' Cassie leaned forward expectantly.

'I trusted Erik with my life and all my knowledge. I had no intention of keeping the real purpose of our trip from him, so I explained, and he understood.' Sir Alric rubbed his face tiredly. 'He was such a promising student.'

'But he died. He died because you found the Urn.'

'Yes.' He gave her a direct, sober stare. 'I never intended him to touch the thing, but I should have anticipated how the Urn would work. He was first to lay eyes on it, and I still remember his extraordinary elation. As I considered how to approach it, and retreated to consult the manuscript, he disobeyed me, and retrieved it himself.'

Cassie bit her lip. 'Why didn't he wait?'

He shrugged. 'Who knows? It was so uncharacteristic of Erik, I can only assume that something besides the Curse that was cast on each of the artefacts was at play. Perhaps if I'd been the one to spot the Urn first, I could have resisted its spell far better than poor Erik.'

'Or maybe not,' said Cassie dryly. 'And if you'd touched the Urn first, the Curse would have struck you. And I hate to think where *that* would have led, with a spirit as powerful as yours.' She shuddered, remembering the look in Ranjit's eyes when he was under the Pendant's curse at the Hagia Sophia.

'That's true,' Sir Alric said. 'And I dread to think of it too. If you'd known Erik, you'd understand what a shock it was. To see him go in an instant from a gentle, intelligent boy to a murderous, brutal . . . monster, is the only word. There was almost nothing of Erik left.'

Cassie swallowed. *Almost nothing of him left . . .*

But Ranjit *had* regained himself. Ranjit had escaped the Curse, she'd made sure of that. He'd regained his sanity, she knew that when she saw him for that last time in Istanbul. But how must he feel now as he went on the run, lost and alone, knowing what he had done?

No. She couldn't let herself think about it. She'd find him – she'd help him. But first things first. She returned to the conversation. 'And what about the landslide that killed Erik?'

Sir Alric gave an exhausted sigh. 'There was no landslide. I tried to restrain him every way I knew how. I thought I was strong, but I was nothing compared to Erik

63

with a Few Curse on him. I had to kill him, Cassie. I had to kill the brightest and best of my students, and I have never forgiven myself for it.'

There was genuine pain on Sir Alric's face, and it was such an alien sight Cassie had to look away. 'But you took the Urn,' she said softly.

'Yes. The Curse spent itself on Erik, and it would have seemed a waste of all that had happened if I'd left it where it was – unsafe, un-cursed, and there for Brigitte to find whenever she finally worked it out. I couldn't leave it. I took it back to the Academy, kept it safe – but I never did find the other artefacts.'

Cassie raised her eyebrows. 'But they were found.'

'Brigitte must have had some access to the contents of the first half of the manuscript, before I discovered it myself. It was her daughter Katerina who tracked down the Knife in Cambodia, but she must have allowed Keiko to retrieve it, to touch it first. Clever of her, and malicious. Keiko was never quite my favourite student, but the way the Knife affected her . . .' He shrugged. 'I wish I had realised sooner what the Svenssons were up to.'

Cassie rose and paced the room, thinking. 'So what did Brigitte *want* with the artefacts? Did you ever find out? I can understand her wanting the Knife – I've seen what it can do to other Few – and I see the point of the Pendant, too. It sort of . . .' She hesitated, clearing her throat. 'It sort of allowed Ranjit to have a similar power to me, projecting his spirit's power outside of himself. But why would she want the Urn? The Eldest made that so he could feed from other spirits. That's a weird thing to want to do, and surely only he could do it, as the Eldest. It's not as if Brigitte ever goes hungry – she can overpower a normal human no problem.' And more besides. Cassie shuddered, remembering the horror of the Living Soil she'd encountered in New York, and the human beings Brigitte had imprisoned there, buried alive for her pleasure.

'I don't know why she wanted it,' Sir Alric said. 'But I'm as certain as I can be that I don't want her to have it. The Urn, I believe, is the most dangerous artefact of them all.'

Cassie looked at him, alarmed. 'Why?'

'It's more a feeling, an innate certainty, Cassie. But that feeling is borne out by the strength of the Curse that was laid on it. It seemed as though the Elders did *not* want anyone who found it to be sane enough to use it.'

There was a cold feeling in the pit of Cassie's stomach. She could hardly imagine a Curse worse than the one that had struck Ranjit.

'No wonder you were so angry,' she murmured.

He furrowed his brow. 'I beg your pardon?'

'When I let Ranjit get away with the Urn.'

'Yes.' He gave her a stern look. 'Yes, I was angry. But it can't be helped now. We just have to hope that Ranjit keeps it safe until he can be located. I don't know precisely what the Urn can do, but it's potentially a huge threat to the Few. And through them, to the rest of humanity.'

They were silent for a moment, each wrapped in their own thoughts. At last Cassie took her seat again, and looked up at him.

'I have something to ask you.'

He raised an eyebrow. 'You, Cassie Bell, never seem to have anything to *ask* me. You tend to tell me.'

She gave a light shrug, and made herself hold his gaze. He remained standing. Clenching her fists below the table, she took a deep breath.

'The Knife. The Pendant. You still have those. And you can use them to sever me from Estelle.'

He stared at her as if, frankly, it was Cassie who was mad. 'What I *can* do and what I *will* do, Miss Bell, are not the same thing at all.'

She stood up, walked closer to him, and leaned her fists on the desk for support. 'You told me it wasn't possible. It *is*. It's what Ranjit had hoped to do when he did what he did – when he went after the artefacts and ended up being cursed by the Pendant. And it's my decision, not yours!'

'That's where you're wrong. I'm sorry, Cassie, but I've told you this before. My responsibility is to your spirit as much as it is to you. And I will not destroy a Few spirit for your convenience.'

'My . . . *convenience*?' She gaped at him, feeling rage begin to rise inside her. 'Did anyone consider my convenience when they foisted the old bat on me?'

'You know precisely how much I regret that. And yet I still won't reverse it at Estelle's cost. Cassie.' He faced her properly, leaning on the opposite side of the desk. 'You know what I want, and what your spirit wants. It makes so much more sense than this half-life for both of you. *Allow Estelle to enter you completely*, and most of your problems will be solved.'

Rage choked her throat. 'Except the fact that while I'm Few, friends of mine end up dead, or drained, or mad? Except for that?'

'Cassie. You make a fine member of the Few, and I admit I was wrong in my original opinions regarding your suitability for this life. If I can change my opinions, can you not adjust yours? You know there are many fine individuals in the Few, along with the rogues.'

'If I'm Few, I can never be with Ranjit. You said it yourself!'

'It's most unlikely you'll ever be with him anyway,' he said dismissively. 'And we've all made sacrifices. Accept your destiny, Cassie! Why wouldn't you? It is a fine one, it is an honour!'

Cassie guffawed. 'It may be a *fine* one,' she retorted, 'but it isn't what I *want*. I won't do it.'

He sighed. 'I will convince you, Cassie. I *will*, because there's no alternative. I will not condemn Estelle to death or the void.'

Something stirred inside her that wasn't anger. Something that was half her, but half not: it was, of course, Estelle. Cassie could sense the spirit's hope and happiness at hearing Sir Alric defend her.

Yes! Yes, my dear Cassandra, he's right!

Damn them both!

'You are wasting your time! Your time – my time – *Estelle's* time! I will *not* join with her! If you're so worried about it, find her another host. I want rid of her!' The rage was a coruscating thing in her chest, his blank refusal like fuel on a fire. Around her, the room had begun to turn red as the mist of Few-rage descended. Her eyes burned with it.

'You know better by now!' Sir Alric's shout of cold

anger brought her momentarily back to her senses. 'No, Cassie, you will control yourself as I've taught you.'

Breathing hard, she blinked the fire from her eyes. Her trembling limbs began to still as her beating heart calmed.

'No,' she growled at last. 'I won't lose control. I won't use this *power* that was forced on me, which you think I should be happy about. But I will *not* do what you want. Not ever.' She stood up, tall and defiant. 'So you'd better think of something else, Sir Alric. And fast. I don't want this sprit inside me any more.'

The headmaster did not speak for a long time. He walked behind his desk and slid open a drawer, removing a file and flicking through it. Cassie wasn't sure if he was doing something constructive or simply playing for time.

'Sit down, Cassie.' He sat down and gestured at the chair opposite his own.

'No thanks.'

He took a breath, but clearly decided not to argue further. His fingers trembled slightly as he flicked through documents, finally pulling one out and laying it on top of the pile.

'The Urn.' He pressed his fingertips on the desk and looked up at her, his eyes granite-hard. 'It was created by the Eldest as an evil kind of feeding-trough. He would preserve other spirits in it, and feed on them.'

'Yes,' she said impatiently. 'I told you, I know that part.'

'Its original purpose means it has a separate, unintended function. The Urn can contain spirits indefinitely, and not just for feeding. It preserves them in their out-of-body state. Do you see?'

'Yes . . .'

'It could preserve Estelle's, until another host is found.'

Cassie was silenced as thoughts raced round her skull. Of course, *of course*. How could she have forgotten that function of the Urn? It had been what Ranjit intended when he stole the evil thing. The solution was so simple, so elegant. 'But that's . . . that's ideal! It's perfect!'

'Not exactly.' Darke's lips thinned. 'We aren't actually in possession of the Urn. If you recall.'

Cassie nodded, silent for once. Another in the mounting list of reasons she needed to find Ranjit. 'I . . . I can find him,' she said, her voice quieter now.

'Is that so, Cassie?' He closed the file with a snap. 'Do you know something I do not? Have you heard from Ranjit?'

She shook her head, and Sir Alric raised an eyebrow.

'Honestly, I wish I had,' she said. 'But I will, I know I

can get to him if only he'd . . . I can do this. I'll track Ranjit down, and the Urn, and then we'll do exactly what you say. Everyone's happy.'

'No.'

She stiffened. 'No?'

'Do you think it will be so easy to find him? In the state in which he left, after all that he has done? What makes you so sure he would want to be found by you? Perhaps, at last, he may have heeded my warnings about the two of you being together.'

Bastard, she thought. She had to restrain herself from saying it out loud.

'I'm sure,' she said quietly. 'Perhaps you don't because maybe you've never been in love. I'm *sure*.'

Sir Alric studied her for a moment before he spoke again. 'I have been trying to locate Ranjit myself. I've used every resource available to me. Last month I tracked him as far as Belgium; that's where the trail went cold. But I assure you, *I* will find him. *You*, on the other hand, should not even try. It's too dangerous – and frankly, so are you. I have influential Few contacts, and this has to be done with subtlety and guile, not a fist in anyone's face.' His gaze softened. 'Put it out of your head, Cassie. Let me deal with it. After that, we can see what happens. And that is my condition for considering this solution.'

She watched his face, thinking furiously, her fingernails tapping rapidly on the desk. At last she pushed herself up and away from it.

'Fine,' she said finally. 'We have a deal.'

CHAPTER SIX

Cassie found each day at the Academy was dragging unbearably. Unable to concentrate in any of her classes, she could think only of the quiet hours when she could get back to her room and get to her laptop. Yet when she was there, clicking on page after page and discussion thread after thread, she lived in a world of frustration.

Of course she hadn't kept her promise to Sir Alric – actually, she told herself, she'd been careful not to give him one. As if she could go blithely about her school life without joining the hunt for Ranjit! Ranjit *and* the Urn, she reminded herself, because the Urn was almost as important as he was. Without it, they could never be together anyway. The Urn was key to everything.

She spent every evening, into the small hours, surfing websites and logging on to networks known only to the Few. This one, she thought as she logged on under yet another pseudonym, seemed more promising than most – but how much was *that* worth? She was growing tired of 'subtlety and guile', as Sir Alric so lightly called it. She was tired of being 'darpak_mumbai' online, tired of pretending to be an older cousin of Ranjit's who'd been to the Academy himself, but simply lost touch with the family. She felt like hitting the caps-lock button and screaming, into the virtual air, 'WHERE IS RANJIT SINGH?'

Cassie restrained herself. Instead she typed in questions that were casual, almost light-hearted: you know a handsome boy from India? Ranjit Singh – joined the Few in his second year at the Academy . . . A powerful spirit? In his fifth year at the school by now, darpak_mumbai guessed. How was he doing? What was he up to these days? He'd seen a statement from the Academy saying Ranjit was on extended study leave? Does anyone know where he might have gone to study?

She'd questioned Few members in Delhi, St Petersburg, Reykjavik, Cairo. Nothing doing. Rubbing her tired eyes one late evening, when she'd missed dinner yet again, she clicked back on to Facebook for a while, taking a much-needed break to catch up with Patrick Malone and the Cranlake Crescent crowd; after all, she was determined not to lose touch with her friend again. He was the one solid point of reference in her life, she thought fondly.

Still, she couldn't resist the call of the Few networks for long. Twenty minutes and some very light gossip later, she was back on that discussion thread, amused to discover her own real name mentioned more than once. Three of the forum members were chattering inconsequentially, but illuminatingly.

> So what's happening with the famous Scholarship Girl?

> I lost track after graduation

> Who?????

> Cassie Bell. Freaky Few is what u mean, cairo_ruthie!

> Oh yeah. The scourge of New York! What's she up to?

> Dunno! Academy's in Kenya this year.

> Somebody warn the lions! Lol!

Well, Cassie thought with a wry grin, at least she'd achieved fame at last. And the gossip and ribbing had an element of respect, which was more than she'd once hoped for. She paused for a moment, fingers over the keyboard.

> *darpak_mumbai has signed in*

> Hey darpak, hows it going?

> Hi darpak, u're back!

> Hello there. No news of ranjit the rake yet?

> Ha, no! Havent heard from him.

Cassie shook her head grimly.

> Ok guys. Will u let me know if u hear anything?

> Sure! Or u could try following trail of sobbing women!

> Lol ruthie! Bye darpak!

Yeah, yeah, lol yourself, Cassie thought bitterly, logging out. She was about to send the laptop to sleep when a small window popped up in the top right-hand corner.

Tiger_eye has sent you a private message.

Biting her lip, Cassie clicked it.

> Hey darpak_mumbai, u still there?

She hesitated, hope leaping.

> Hi. Yes, I'm here.

> Oh good. Didn't want to talk in chatroom

> Yes?

A long pause.

> You're looking for ranjit singh, right?

Cassie enlarged the private window, peering at the avatar. It was the generic silhouette that meant the user hadn't uploaded a photo yet.

> Yes, u know him?

> Used to.

> U know where he is . . . Cassie deleted that quickly.
> U know what he's up to?

> Not sure what he's up to these days.

So why PM her? The frustration was killing Cassie, but

76

she held on to her temper and typed again.

> That's a shame. I'd love to get in touch. Been too long.

The message screen stayed blank for so long, she wanted to put a fist through the laptop.

> Well, officially he's on gap year.

Cassie shut her eyes tight, clenching her fists. *Don't scare them off* . . . > Yes, so I understand. Have you seen him around? Where are you located? If she bit her lip any harder, Cassie thought, she'd draw blood.

>>>>

>>>>

> U still there?

> Yeah. Might be able to help u.

> Great!

>>>>

> Are you there? Cassie was rocking back and forth in her chair now, chewing her fingers.

> Got to go. Will be in touch OK?

> OK . . . Where are u based? Have you spoken to Ranjit?

>>>>

>>>>

>>>>

Tiger_eye is no longer online

Cassie gave a strangled scream of frustration and banged her forehead with her fists. It was the first time she'd had even a hint of a clue, and whoever this was, they were no longer online. And who called themselves Tiger_eye anyway, she thought with annoyance? Why wouldn't they let on their location? Well, that was easily checked. She clicked on the name and brought up Tiger_eye's profile.

This account has been deactivated

What? Startled, she pushed her chair back from the desk. Deactivated? In the last thirty seconds?

Tiger_eye . . .

Something constricted her throat, and she blinked. Could it be? Could it have been *Ranjit*?

Who else would choose a name that told nothing – but that would mean something to Cassie? It wasn't compulsory but it was good etiquette on the network to give some indication of place and identity – if the Few couldn't trust each other, or so the theory went, nobody could. So why be so secretive?

Tiger_eye

He used to laugh when she told him he had 'eyes like a bloody tiger' when he was cross. But how would he know 'darpak_mumbai' was her? Maybe from her IP address . . . ? Her heart leaped. The reticence of the user seemed right. It all seemed to fit. Ranjit wouldn't want to reveal himself, wouldn't want to give any clue to his identity. He probably wouldn't even want to show himself to Cassie, but maybe he hadn't been able to help himself. Their spirits were so tightly bound and connected.

And then he'd panicked and logged off.

Cassie's heart thudded in her ribcage. She shouldn't allow herself to hope, but she couldn't help it. It all made so much sense. And at least it was a start.

Feeling suddenly far more hopeful, if still troubled, Cassie shut down the laptop, yawning. Two in the morning, again. No wonder she couldn't focus in class. No wonder some of the teachers were getting unusually stroppy with her. At least tomorrow was Saturday.

She fell gratefully into the comfortable bed, only just remembering to draw the mosquito drapes, and for the first time in weeks she slept through the night, undisturbed except for some *very* pleasant dreams of Ranjit returning to her . . .

When she did wake, it was to the bright morning sun streaming through the open windows, and the sounds of daytime birds and vervet monkeys in the trees. Pushing herself up, she blinked and shoved hair out of her eyes.

'Oh, Cassie,' said a familiar voice. 'I hope I didn't wake you . . .'

Cassie flushed, hoping she hadn't given away anything about what she'd been dreaming. Isabella was sitting at her desk, half-turned to Cassie with an anxious expression on her face.

'No. No, of course not.' Cassie peered stupidly at her watch. 'You're up?'

Not just up, she thought, but wide awake. Grief had affected Isabella in many ways, but she had never been a morning person. Yet there she sat, alert and solemn, and the printer was already humming busily.

'I had to write a letter,' said Isabella. 'I couldn't stay in bed.'

'What kind of a letter?' Cassie climbed out of bed and stretched. 'Are you OK?'

Isabella nodded, forcing a smile. 'I'm OK. More OK now, anyway.'

Cassie went over to her, uneasy, and laid a hand on her shoulder. Isabella had never been anything approaching fat, but the thinness and fragility of her bones were a shock now, every time Cassie touched her. There were telltale tracks on her face, still visible although the tears had long dried. Nervously Cassie ventured, 'Why more OK now?'

'Because I've made a decision.' Isabella turned completely to face her. 'I've written to Sir Alric. Here.' She pulled the sheet from the printer. 'I'm . . . I'm leaving the Academy.'

Cassie felt as if someone had punched her in the stomach. She sat down, abruptly, on Isabella's bed. 'No.'

'Yes. I'm sorry, Cassie. I really am. My decision's final.'

'Isabella!' Cassie felt tears sting her eyes; she didn't for an instant think Isabella was bluffing. 'I'm sorry, I . . . look, I know I've been preoccupied the last couple of weeks. I know I haven't spent enough time with you—'

'Oh, don't talk nonsense, Cassie Bell!' Isabella came and sat down on the bed beside her, clasping her hand. 'You've been brilliant. Truly. And I know you've been preoccupied too, and I'm sorry I haven't talked to you more about all of this, but . . . I've been thinking. Thinking about everything. And this is the right thing. For me, at least. You'll find another feeding source, I know you will.' Her face was suddenly anxious. 'Won't you?'

'Oh for heaven's sake! That's not the issue! It doesn't matter a damn!'

'It *does*, Cassie. But you'll be all right, I know you will. Otherwise I wouldn't go, no matter what. And you know we're going to be friends forever, no?'

'Isabella,' she whispered. 'Of course I know that. But

81

what will I do without you, here at the Academy? When are you going?'

'As soon as possible.' Isabella squeezed her hand. 'Oh, Cassie, I'll miss you so much. You'll be OK, won't you?'

Cassie felt a tear roll down her cheek. 'Of course. You need to do what's best for you, I know that. But Isabella, have you talked to your parents about this?' A tiny spark of hope burned, and was instantly extinguished when Isabella nodded.

'Yes, and they've agreed to it. I'm sorry, Cassie. There's no point me staying. It's not just that it's so painful for me – the thing is, I'm not even managing to learn anything. I can't think about anything but . . . well, all that's happened here.' She sighed. 'I need a new start. A new place.'

Cassie knew how that felt, even more so now. She rubbed her eyes, trying to wipe her tears away. 'I do understand, Isabella. Honestly. It's just a bit of a shock, that's all.'

'I'm sorry . . .'

'Stop saying that.' Cassie returned her hug, fiercely. 'Don't you dare apologise. If this is right for you, you have to do it.'

'Know what, Cassie Bell?' There were tears in Isabella's

eyes again too. 'I knew you'd understand. I knew you would. That's why I love you.'

'Shut up and stop making me cry, you awful Argentinean cow!'

Isabella laughed. It was a feeble and slightly hysterical sound, but God, thought Cassie, it was a good one.

She *did* understand. It made sense for Isabella to leave, however dreadful that would be for Cassie. Feeding was the least of it; after all, Sir Alric would organise an alternative, no doubt some poor first or second year who would drink the Few drink and then forget what had happened.

But Cassie wasn't losing a feeding source. She was losing her best friend, her ally, the girl who had taken care of her from the moment she'd arrived at the Academy. She was losing one of the two most important people in her world.

And how ironic that, just as she thought she might be closer to finding Ranjit, she should have to lose Isabella.

'I'm going to tell him.' Isabella stood up, but she held on to Cassie's hands. 'I'm going up to Sir Alric's office now.'

'Do you want me to come with you?' Cassie squeezed her hands, knowing how daunting a prospect it must be.

Isabella shook her head. 'I'll be OK. Wish me luck?'

'I would never wish you anything else,' she said, standing up to hug her friend again. 'And you won't need it. He'll understand. But good luck anyway.'

Cassie stared at the door as it closed behind her friend, her heart sinking further in her chest with each passing moment.

CHAPTER SEVEN

'Cassie!' Richard rose from the gym bench and laid down his fencing mask and épée. He clasped her hand and pulled her down beside him. 'Is it true? About Isabella?'

It never failed to amaze her how fast news travelled in the Academy. She was glad Richard had grabbed her before anyone else could buttonhole her and demand information, especially since she could now focus on him and ignore the sneers of Saski and Sara.

'It's true,' she said quietly. 'She's leaving.'

'God, Cassie.' Richard reached round and squeezed her shoulders. 'That's a real blow. I'm so sorry.'

'It's a blow for us, but it's right for her.' She tried to give him a smile. 'She's made the decision she needs to make. And it's not like she's vanishing off the face of the earth.'

'Can you *imagine*?' Sara's brittle tones drifted across

from the piste, where she was fiddling with the fastening of her neck guard. Deliberately slowly, Cassie guessed, so that her words would be loud and clear. 'Have you ever heard of anyone leaving the Academy? For the sake of some dead trailer-trash boy?'

Cassie gasped, then frowned and tried to get up, but Richard reached up and grabbed her hand again, drawing her firmly back down.

'It's what she wants, C. You know it is.'

'Then that little hussy should be careful what she wishes for,' hissed Cassie with a glare at Sara, but she subsided on to the bench once more. 'I know you're right. But I still want to turn her oesophagus inside out.'

'Of course you do, love,' crooned Richard in his calm-down-Cassie voice. 'And visually that would be a vast improvement, but we've got to be the bigger people here, right?'

Cassie spluttered a laugh, earning a furious glare from Sara that gave her almost as much satisfaction as a solid punch would have.

'I still can't quite believe it, though,' murmured Richard bleakly. 'This old place won't be the same without Bella Isabella.'

'To put it mildly,' Cassie said then paused, looking up as someone came over to them. 'Hey, Ayeesha.'

The Bajan girl sat down at Cassie's other side, tugging off her fencing glove, then running a hand through her braids. 'God, that Sara. What a bitch, huh? So it's true? Isabella's really leaving?'

Cassie sighed. She knew Ayeesha meant well, but she was already tired of talking about it, and way too miserable.

Ayeesha patted her thigh. 'I'm sorry. I understand. It's just that it's so unexpected.'

'Not really,' put in Richard protectively, 'when you think about it. It took guts for Isabella to come back at all this term.'

'Cormac's devastated. I think he's half in love with her,' added Ayeesha with mock-indignation.

Cassie managed a grin. 'As if he'd dare, girl.'

'True. Anyway, you and Isabella should come and sit with us at lunch. I'd love to see her, and otherwise you'll get stuck with a bunch of nosy parkers pumping her for information. OK?'

'Thanks, Ayeesha,' said Cassie gratefully.

'Richard can come too, if he behaves.' She grinned over at him.

'No chance of that, gorgeous,' Richard retorted. 'But I'll join you anyway. Cassie, you look like you could do with blowing off some steam. *En garde!*' He stood up abruptly.

Cassie followed him to the piste, noting that he'd

rescued her in the nick of time from an advancing trio of curious but disappointed classmates. They sat down on the bench she and Richard had vacated, muttering darkly.

'You're a gent, Richard. A gent with great timing.' She slipped on her mask and lifted her weapon.

'I may be a gentleman, but I'm still going to thrash you fifteen–nil,' he told her equably.

'In your dreams, Halton-Jones.'

'Ha! I bet you haven't practised all summer.'

'Yeah, well they're not big on fencing at Cranlake Crescent. It's more of a concealed knife thing,' she said with a wry laugh. 'But we do know how to deal with public schoolboys.' She drew her mask down, and thought yet again, Thank God for Richard.

Not that she'd go any easier on him. She took up her position and saluted, glad for the distraction.

'*En garde*, posh boy!'

Evening fell so swiftly here on the Equator. Cassie leaned on the windowsill in their quarters and gazed out at the indigo night, listening to the high chirruping chorus of tree frogs and cicadas, louder even than the ocean. She could make out a few students in the grounds below; talking, laughing, drinking; some of them stealing a kiss or three. She didn't feel like joining them down there, even when she saw a small knot of her favourite Few members clustered at a table with some sneaky cocktails in the light of an elaborately carved lantern.

Ayeesha and Cormac had been true to their word at lunchtime in the dining room, sitting at a table that accommodated only five, and glaring away anyone who dared come near Isabella. Cassie was beyond grateful, but she didn't want to socialise tonight, even with them.

There were many Few she liked, but for the most part their friendship suddenly didn't seem to matter as much any more. Who knew if they'd even remain friends if she managed to accomplish her wish to get rid of Estelle? Cassie sighed. She was going to miss Isabella desperately.

But she couldn't deny it: now that the decision had been taken, her roommate seemed more at ease, far calmer. She was sitting at her desk, writing cards with a fancy calligraphy pen – must be to elderly relatives in Argentina or something, breaking the news that she was leaving her prestigious school. Feeling Cassie's gaze on her, Isabella glanced up and smiled.

'This is the worst part,' she said, nodding at a card that was still resolutely blank inside. 'Tato and Tata. They'll be so disappointed. Tata's brother was a graduate of the

Academy himself.' She sighed. 'But she'll understand, I think. At least the hard part's over.'

'You mean, telling Sir Alric? I thought you said he didn't take it so badly?'

'No. He was not nearly as scary as I expected. It was thinking about it that was the worst part; but he was really very understanding, Cassie. I suppose he knew he was never going to convince me otherwise.'

'Hm. I'm sure you're right.' Given her own longing for Isabella to stay, even with all that had happened, Cassie had imagined Sir Alric would be more determined to try and cajole a last-minute change of heart. He wouldn't be keen for a student to leave the Academy, especially under circumstances that could expose some of its darker underbelly . . . But in a way, Cassie thought his calm response was for the best. The decision had come too hard to Isabella and her friends for the headmaster to start giving her a hard time.

An abrupt knock on the door interrupted her thoughts, and Cassie jumped.

'Can you get that? I'm struggling with this card . . .' Isabella chewed her pen and shoved her fingers through her hair.

Cassie yanked the door open, and frowned as she saw who stood there.

Speak of the devil.

'Good evening, Cassie.' Sir Alric's face gave nothing away; he was as coolly charming as he always was on official business.

She bit back a '*What do you want?*' After all, if she was right about his intentions, then she wanted the same thing too . . . her wishes, for once, might be coinciding with his.

'Evening, Sir Alric,' Cassie said pointedly, so Isabella could hear. 'What can we do for you?'

Isabella turned in her seat, a little alarmed, but Sir Alric smiled at her directly.

'I have something I need to discuss with Isabella. With both of you, in fact.'

'Right . . .' Cassie stared at him, trying to get a read on his plan.

'I know it's a little late, but this is important.'

Folding her arms, she leaned on the doorframe. 'Go on.'

He shook his head a little and took a step back from the doorway. 'I can't explain here, but I must ask you both to come with me.'

'*Now?*'

'Now, Cassie.' He looked past her and nodded at Isabella. 'This won't take long.'

What's he up to? thought Cassie, as she waited for Isabella to replace the cap on her expensive pen and join them. If he was going to attempt to convince Isabella to stay at the Academy, why couldn't he just do it there? Maybe this wasn't what she thought it was. Perhaps he had some less benevolent means of convincing students not to leave . . . She shook her head. That was ridiculous. Though stranger things had happened around there. She went on her guard as Isabella joined them by the door.

But as they stepped into the corridor another idea slid into Cassie's head; she felt her heart jolt again, though for different reasons. Could he . . . could he possibly have news of Ranjit? If he did, could it be bad news? Maybe that's why he wanted Isabella there, in case Cassie reacted badly? A knot began to form in Cassie's stomach. She didn't like all this mysteriousness.

'It's flattering you came yourself, sir,' she said tightly. 'Why haven't you sent your attack dog?'

Sir Alric closed the door behind them and led them both away. 'You mean Marat? Ah, what a shame you're so hostile, Cassie.' He smiled a little. 'You wouldn't believe it, I know, but Marat is a treasure house of Few lore and knowledge. I know you dislike him, but he's always been loyal to me, and I've never had reason to doubt him. You should have a more open mind about those you encounter – especially amongst the Few,' he added pointedly.

Isabella was silent, anxious, but Cassie scowled. 'If you trust him so completely, why *didn't* you send him to get us?'

'There are some things I don't even want to share with Marat. At the present time, anyway.'

Now Cassie's curiosity was piqued even more. Marat must know about Isabella leaving the Academy. Information about Ranjit, on the other hand – that could be something Sir Alric would want to keep under his hat.

Isabella was hanging back a little, so Cassie took the chance to hiss at him, 'What's going on? Is this something to do with Ranjit? Why is Isabella coming?'

'Patience, Cassie.' He gave her a strict sidelong glare, and spoke in a normal voice that Isabella must have heard. 'This concerns Isabella more than anyone.'

Maybe he *was* going to try to talk her out of it. She turned back and exchanged a worried glance with Isabella. Darke needn't think he was going to use Cassie's feeding to blackmail Isabella into staying. Cassie wasn't going to stand for that. She hoped her friend knew it, and tried a smile to reassure her. What was he up to?

Cassie blinked as Sir Alric turned to climb yet another

flight of stairs. 'Er . . . but your office is on this floor?'

'We're not going to my office. Do stop trying to second-guess me, Miss Bell.'

More irritated than ever, she followed him up the next flight and along another narrow corridor. They were in a separate part of the building now – one with so many twists and turns along the way, she was no longer sure where they were heading, and Isabella had caught up, nervous, sticking close to Cassie.

'Where are we going?' she hissed.

Cassie could only shake her head. Her fists were balled – partly with aggravation, partly because she was tensed for fight or flight. Where the hell was he taking them?

Cassie glanced to left and right, seeking a quick exit. Even with all that was going on, her Few instincts were kicking in. But what could she do – simply grab Isabella and abseil with her out of a top-floor window? And go where? Cassie shook her head. Whatever Sir Alric's intentions were, they were about to find out, because there was nowhere for them to go. This new passageway led only to a single, thick wooden door.

As Sir Alric drew a key from his pocket, Cassie swallowed hard. It was a heavy, elaborate thing, carved with the same Few symbols that she'd spotted on pillars and the corners of paintings everywhere in this school;

the same kind of symbol that was burned into her own shoulder blade, though in broken form. Cassie found she was holding her breath as Sir Alric turned the key in the lock, and then swung the door open.

The room was plain, furnished only with a bed and a couple of armchairs, and lined with books. And strangely, the first thing that hit her was the fresh coastal air, scented with oleander and seaweed and salt, borne in through the open French windows, light curtains billowing in the gentle breeze.

She simply didn't believe what she was seeing; the apparent delusion was too crazy. Beside her, Isabella gave a hoarse cry, and stumbled against her. Cassie caught her in her arms, but could do nothing but stare at the figure that stood in the centre of the room.

He watched them gravely, apprehensively, one hand gripping his wrist tightly as if to hold himself still.

Jake Johnson.

CHAPTER EIGHT

They stood immobile for what felt like minutes, but could only have been seconds. Jake did not seem to be breathing any more than Cassie was; Isabella was gasping for air, stunned almost senseless, weak in Cassie's arms. Cassie thought she might actually faint.

Then Isabella tensed, breathing hard and audibly as she recovered. She drew away from Cassie, and took a cautious step towards Jake. Then she took another, studying his face with disbelieving hope.

Her next step brought her close enough to the boy to touch him, and she did, reaching out shaking fingers to his cheek. She almost flinched as she made contact with his skin, as if expecting it to be stone cold, but at her touch he made a slight sound, and she pressed her palms fiercely to his cheeks.

'Jake . . .' she breathed.

The next moment, Isabella had flung herself into his embrace, wrapping her arms round his neck, sobbing his name. He closed his arms round her, so tightly Cassie thought he'd crush her, but she didn't protest, just held him all the closer.

'Jake! *Jake!* Is it really you?'

'It's me, it's me.' His voice was muffled in her hair, and Cassie suspected she could see a tear run from his eye. She could only stare at her reunited friends, her heart thundering. She couldn't look at Sir Alric. What kind of a game was he playing? This was crazy. Jake was *alive* this whole time?

After what seemed like forever, Jake gently pulled away from Isabella, though he kept his hands on her shoulders, staring at her like he'd never look away.

'Cassie?' He glanced over with a weak smile. 'Cassie, it's so good to see you too.'

Unfolding her stiff arms, she walked forward and hugged him hard. 'Jake. What the hell?'

'I'm sorry. I'm so very sorry,' he murmured.

Cassie stood back, eyeing him, unable to repress her growing, disbelieving smile. 'I . . . I can't believe this . . .' She tailed off and her smile began to fade as anger took over. 'But it's not you who owes us an apology.' She turned on her heel and stared at Sir Alric.

He was still just inside the door, watching them. 'Despite that, Cassie, I think I'll allow Jake to explain. I'm sure you'd rather hear it from him.'

He's right, she thought. She wasn't sure she wanted to hear a word out of his mouth right now. Cassie turned back to Jake and Isabella, whose face was still buried in Jake's neck, her arms wrapped around his body.

'OK, what . . .' Cassie stopped, tried again. 'What happened? How did you . . . ?' She faltered again, unsure of where to start.

'Why don't we all sit down?' Jake said, clearing his throat. 'I think we all need to.'

'God, it all makes sense now. We both saw something. Isabella and I, we both saw a figure on that balcony.' Her hands still trembling around her glass of water, Cassie nodded towards the French windows. 'It was you, wasn't it? You must have seen us.'

Jake nodded slowly, his hands constantly stroking Isabella's hair. She was sitting on his lap, her face stained with tears of shock and happiness, her arms around his shoulders. Sir Alric had not taken a seat; he stood with his back to the bookshelves, watching them all in silence.

'I'm so sorry. I wanted to yell to you, of course I did.'

He glanced at Sir Alric. 'But it wasn't allowed. I'd made a promise and I had to keep it.'

'That wouldn't have stopped you before.' Cassie gave Sir Alric a vicious look. 'What did he threaten you with?'

'It wasn't like that, Cassie.' Jake smiled soberly. 'A lot . . . a lot has happened since Istanbul. A lot of it I wasn't aware of, obviously, but some of it I was. We've had a lot of time to talk.' His eyes met Sir Alric's, but without a trace of their usual hostility.

'Then *tell* us. What happened? Why all the secrecy?'

'Yes, Jake,' Isabella said, her voice low and trembling, hardly able to stop it breaking. 'Please, tell us what happened. How . . . how are you alive?'

'He wasn't,' murmured Sir Alric. 'At least, he was close enough to death that it made no difference.'

Jake swallowed and nodded. 'Sir Alric saved me. That night at the Hagia Sophia, he used . . . some kind of medicine. Something old. Something long past its sell-by date, if you ask me.' He attempted a weak smile. 'I didn't know what he'd done, of course. He told me this later. Weeks later, when I recovered consciousness.'

'Medicine?' Cassie said the word slowly, then furrowed her brow at Sir Alric. 'You didn't . . . Did you use the—'

'The Tears, Cassie, yes. Almost all that were left.'

She stared at him, stunned. She knew just how valuable

and rare the Tears were to the Few. And how irreplaceable . . .

As if reading her thoughts, Sir Alric grunted dismissively. 'I decided the Few owed as much to Jake and his family. Call it payback, if you like.'

Feeling sudden tears of surprise and grudging gratitude spring to her eyes, Cassie blinked hard. She wasn't going to cry, no way – but it was all so overwhelming. 'Thank you,' she said quietly, gazing at Sir Alric very directly. 'I know how much that means. I know what you've . . . given up.'

He nodded in acknowledgement.

'Thank you from me, too,' blurted Isabella, detaching her arms from Jake long enough to extend a hand to her headmaster. A little surprised, he clasped it. 'You don't know how I— This means more than— Oh, *Jake*.' And then she was in her boyfriend's arms again, kissing and hugging him.

Sir Alric gave Cassie a wry look, and she moved away to stand next to him while the two others embraced. 'I feel quite the gooseberry,' he murmured.

'No kidding.' She raised an eyebrow. 'But thank you. Really. I know what the Tears were worth.'

'To the Few, yes.' He shrugged.

Jake eventually disentangled himself from Isabella and

took a deep breath. 'I'm sorry we couldn't say anything before. I didn't want to get you into any more trouble – and if you knew I was still alive, there *would* be more. That's how it had to be. It was for your safety as well as mine.'

'Oh, Jake.' Isabella took his face in her hands and shook it gently. 'Nothing could have been worse than thinking you were dead. *Nothing*.'

'I know. I'm sorry, sweetheart. I'm so sorry.'

'Jake, your parents . . . do they know . . . ?' Cassie asked hesitantly.

'No.' He shook his head quickly, looking tormented. 'Even they don't know I'm alive. They couldn't. I want to tell them, of course I do, but—' He licked his lips.

Sir Alric took over. 'You have to understand that Jake's survival, and the means employed to achieve it, are very controversial indeed. He'd be a major target – and a very easy one.' He shot Jake an apologetic smile, but Jake only nodded. 'Jake has done a lot to thwart some very evil Few – vengeful ones. I wouldn't want the Svenssons or their allies taking revenge on Jake, or coming after him to get at you. They're more than capable of doing that. Besides, Jake knows far too much about the Few – we're all aware of that, just as we're aware how hostile he's been towards us. If even a small percentage of

Few knew he was still breathing, things wouldn't go on that way for long. And if they knew the *Tears* had been used to save him . . . ?' Sir Alric tailed off, shaking his head grimly. He seemed a little incredulous at his own actions, Cassie thought.

Isabella took a scared breath and hugged Jake even tighter. 'But surely, his parents—'

'If Mom and Dad knew, that would make them a target too,' said Jake flatly. 'They'd never be able to fake it; I know them. They'd let it slip somehow, and the Few – some of them – would use them to get to me.'

'Even before this, I had already heard mutters that Jake's parents ought to be in the Confine because of all that they know,' added Sir Alric. 'And that was from perfectly respectable Council Elders.'

Cassie nodded, silent, twisting her hands together as she thought it over. What Jake and Sir Alric said was true, and she couldn't in all honesty be angry with either of them, however bewildered she felt. The enormity of the risk being taken here was finally catching up with her.

'Wow. I . . . I really can't believe you did this,' Cassie murmured to Sir Alric. Jake and Isabella had returned to silent embrace.

'Well, those two seem sufficiently grateful, wouldn't you say?' He gave a small smile. 'Speaking of romance and deathless love, Miss Bell, I'm a little surprised you haven't asked me yet.'

She blinked. 'What?'

He studied her face keenly. 'You haven't asked me how my hunt for Ranjit is progressing.'

'Oh.' Cassie said. 'No, but . . . ah, have you heard? Anything?'

Tilting his head a little, he continued to watch her. 'Well, I daresay this business with Jake could have driven even Ranjit Singh from your head.'

She could hear the suspicion in his tone, and was indignant despite the fact that he was right in his insinuation that she'd been looking on her own. 'Well. I assumed you'd let me know if you'd heard. Wouldn't you?'

Sir Alric eyed her for a moment. 'The fact is, I *haven't* found anything. But I am continuing to search, Cassie, in every way I know how. I want you to know that. And I especially want you to continue to leave this to me.'

'Of course,' she said innocently.

He frowned, and then turned his attention back to Isabella and Jake. 'I appreciate how happy you all are to be reunited, but we need to talk seriously,' he said.

Jake was instantly attentive; Cassie was almost amused by the American boy's change of attitude. He'd obviously found a new respect for his former headmaster, but that, she thought, was as it should be, after what Sir Alric had done for him.

It didn't mean *she* had to be an obedient and respectful pupil, though . . .

'Jake has to remain in hiding, Isabella,' said Sir Alric. 'As we've said, his appearance would raise too many awkward questions, might bring some very unpleasant creatures out of the woodwork. And for the same reasons, his family must continue to believe him dead. I know that's difficult, but it's unavoidable, for the moment. Besides,' he said, turning to Jake, 'you're still weak. You will need to stay here, in this room and under my supervision, until you're completely recovered.'

'Absolutely *not!*'

They all stared. For the first time, Isabella had jumped up, fired with anger. It did Cassie's heart good to see her friend back to her normal, sparky, positively terrifying self. 'I'm not letting Jake out of my sight again! Not even to stay in this room. I'll look after him! Do you hear me?'

'I expect the whole school can hear you,' muttered Sir Alric, taken aback.

'And I will *not* go calmly back to my classes while he's stuck here. I *will not!*'

Sir Alric sighed deeply, and allowed himself a small

smile. 'But you speak of going back to your classes, Isabella? That at least is very good news. I'd hoped you would stay at the Academy.' He looked from her to Cassie and back again. 'To be brutally honest, it's the only reason I was forced to tell you both about Jake.'

Yes, thought Cassie cynically, that makes sense. And a good way of ensuring she'll stay under your supervision, what with everything she knows.

'Of *course* I go back to my classes!' Isabella was spluttering in fury, tossing her hair. 'Of course I will stay at the Academy *now*. My Jake is here! How could I leave? *How?*'

'Still, Isabella, you have to accept that he mustn't—'

'No! I said not out of my sight! *Ever!* You cannot expect to separate us now?'

'I've got to say, I agree,' said Cassie, grinning.

Silenced, Sir Alric looked helplessly around all three of them.

'Very well.' He took another deep breath and nodded. 'I can understand that you do deserve some time alone, you two. It's not as if Isabella's, ah . . . emotional state has escaped my notice. It's hardly fair that you have grieved for so long under false pretences.'

'Indeed,' agreed Isabella sharply, with a dagger-glare.

'And I am delighted to see you back to your old self,

Miss Caruso,' he added drily. 'I have a proposition to put to you and Jake. I own a safari lodge in the Mount Kenya National Park; it's extremely comfortable.'

'I bet it is,' muttered Cassie.

He ignored her. 'I'd like to send you both there to recuperate, Isabella. I'm sure your roommate Miss Bell will be more than willing to take extra notes in class for you.' Cassie cleared her throat pointedly. 'Meanwhile, you and Jake can spend some time together, relax. I'll even allow you to take the remaining Tears, in case Jake has need of them, but that should not be necessary. With those, you'll be fully equipped to take care of him, Isabella; you'll need nothing else.'

Cassie couldn't help lifting her eyebrows in surprise.

'And Cassie: your class is scheduled for a field trip and game drive there in a week's time, so you'll see your friends again soon.' He shot her a meaningful glance, and she flushed, realising he was thinking of her feeding opportunities. 'Just don't say a word to your classmates – especially not the Few – and keep your visits to Isabella and Jake extremely quiet. Do you all understand?'

'It's perfect.' A grin spread across Isabella's face, all the light and life back in it. 'And Cassie – I think I'll have a little more *energy* from now on.'

Nervously, Cassie glanced at Jake, expecting him to

explode with anger – but he was nodding. Clearly his recent experiences had changed much about his attitudes to the Few. Jake might not be thrilled about the feeding relationship between Cassie and his girlfriend, she thought, but he understood. He even gave her a rueful smile.

'I agree about the safari lodge, Sir Alric,' Jake said. 'It's exactly what Isabella needs.'

'And you!' Isabella tapped his chin with a scolding finger.

'Both of you,' grinned Cassie. 'And I'd say I was going to miss you – but given the situation half an hour ago, I think I can afford to tell you to bugger off for a few weeks!'

CHAPTER NINE

The twin-engined plane was a little bigger than Richard's, and full of her classmates, but Cassie might as well have been alone. She huddled in her seat, staring out of the window at the savannah below, using the landscape and the wildlife, scattered like so many toys across it, as an excuse to be unsociable.

She couldn't help thinking about Ranjit, especially now that Isabella and Jake were so loved-up again. She'd tried many times over the last few days to draw out Tiger_eye again, but whoever it was, they'd been resolutely silent. Nothing else she'd seen or heard discussed in that chatroom or any other had proved such a strong lead. She was certain now that if it wasn't Ranjit, it was certainly a friend of his – someone who could help.

But she was desperate to believe it *was* Ranjit himself.

It was just the sort of thing he would do – he must be very familiar with the Few networks, and he was bound to use them to keep track of anyone who might be hunting for him. And if he suspected she was looking for him – as he surely must – then wouldn't he be tempted to make a tentative contact, even if he later regretted it and went back into hiding? It all made sense.

Now she had to convince him there was no need for him to hide, that he could stop running. She loved him; that was all he needed to know. The whole hideous situation was fixable. All she had to do was tempt him back out of his hidey-hole once more . . .

A friendly elbow nudged her side, and she turned to Richard with a practised smile.

He grinned back. 'Hey, Cassie Bell, you're missing my magnificent flying skills, aren't you?'

She laughed. 'What, the ones that add such excitement to a trip?'

'She's just missing excitement, full stop,' called Cormac from the seat in front. 'Richard, why aren't you showing our friend one of your famous good times?'

For an instant Cassie's eyes locked with Richard's, and he gave her a slightly regretful smile, and her heart turned over. Then, solemnly, he winked.

'Ah, if only,' sighed Richard. 'There's more than that I'd

like to show her . . . But I fear I'm a poor substitute for our bella Isabella.'

Relieved, Cassie returned his elbow-nudge with added force. 'You've got that right!' Richard clutched his side with a grin. 'Gosh, for a moment, it was as if Isabella was right here with me.'

Cassie couldn't help giggling, all the more so when Cormac leaned over the back of his seat to share his latest filthy jokes. She barely listened to the punchlines, but only because she was enjoying the sheer laughter and companionship of the moment.

But in spite of the feeling of camaraderie with the other Few, she knew she'd made her decision, and she was sticking to it. Why else was she tracking Ranjit down so determinedly? She was absolutely certain, more so than she'd been even when she was first initiated into the Few. She would separate herself from Estelle; she would be with Ranjit.

What if he doesn't want you any more?

The small spiteful voice was clear in her head, and Cassie almost smiled to hear it.

Ah, Estelle, she thought sarcastically. Always so encouraging.

Well? Tell me, girl. He ran from you, he's hiding from you. He may not even want to know you any more. And even if he does return, what if why he really loves you, even if he doesn't know it, is because you are one of the Few? You're strong, fearless, beautiful! Perhaps a mere mortal won't quite measure up. You're so much better off with me.

No, Estelle, she thought. No. You're wrong.

We'll see. We'll see how he likes you when you're ordinary. He's Few! He's beautiful, strong and fearless – like you are NOW! Why would he—

'Oh, do shut up,' muttered Cassie aloud.

'Blimey!' said Richard with mock indignation. 'I was only telling you we're coming in to land. I thought you might like to be ready to save our lives, in case there's any turbulence.'

'You are so never going to let me forget that,' she laughed.

'Certainly not. Though I do prefer my superheroes in a bit of Lycra . . .' he retorted with a devilish grin.

Oh, she thought, she would miss her Few friends. There were so many of them she liked and trusted, and she couldn't fool herself that she would see much of them once she was back living a normal, human reality. Would they resent her for getting rid of her spirit? Would they turn their backs on her, or not speak to her again after she'd done it?

The Few were elite, very much a community unto

111

themselves. She might run into them now and again over her lifetime, but she'd never again have this closeness, this easy companionship of people who knew exactly what she was and respected her for it. She'd be giving up friends, a wonderful network, possibly a brilliant and successful future.

Quite, put in Estelle truculently.

Quite, thought Cassie grimly. But look what I'll be gaining: Ranjit. And myself. I'll be getting my *life* back. Estelle was silent, sulking again, but that didn't bother Cassie. She'd rather the old bat kept her trap shut right now. She had more than enough to worry about in one mind.

The plane rumbled smoothly on to a grassy airstrip, and in mere minutes Cassie and her classmates were clambering out, stretching, grabbing their bags, pointing out their luggage to the drivers, laughing and joking and gazing around in delighted awe.

'I am gonna *like* it here,' declared Ayeesha.

'What? Without a branch of Neiman Marcus?' joked Cassie.

'There's one behind those bushes,' announced the Bajan girl airily, pointing vaguely at her surroundings.

Cassie laughed, feeling the piercing regret once more, and just as quickly shooing it away. There was no reason, after all, why she couldn't enjoy her friends' company for now.

'I wish Isabella hadn't left,' sighed Ayeesha, turning gloomy. 'She'd have loved it here. With or without Neiman Marcus.'

Cassie simply nodded, deciding it was better to say nothing than actively lie. The rest of the school had been allowed to think Isabella had indeed left, but they'd find out soon enough that she was staying. Cassie hoped they wouldn't blame her for that secrecy, too.

The camp was not far from the airstrip, and even knowing the extravagances of the Darke Academy, it was not what Cassie had been expecting. When Sir Alric had mentioned tents, she'd rather assumed the students might just be slumming it for once. But these 'tents' were the size of small houses, furnished with everything from desks to baths to elegant beds. Cassie whistled as she gazed around.

'Well, this is rather nice,' announced Alice Pritchard with a raised eyebrow, dumping her Louis Vuitton in one corner of their tent.

Cassie widened her eyes at the English girl in agreement. She'd be sharing with Alice while they stayed here – they were the only two without roommates – but she could live with that. Frankly, she could put up with pretty much anything, she thought, when the living conditions were this luxurious. There were even Persian rugs on the wooden flooring, for heaven's sake.

'Which bed do you fancy, then?' asked Alice. She flopped into a chair and watched Cassie look at the two four-poster beds, each made up with cool Egyptian cotton bedclothes.

'I'm fine with either.' Cassie was a little surprised she was being given a choice, seeing as she'd never really got along with Alice. 'I'll have this one.' She kicked off her sandals and jumped on to the nearest bed with a flourish.

Alice laughed back – a genuine laugh, Cassie thought – before growing serious again. 'Listen, Cassie . . . I'm sorry about Isabella,' the English girl said softly. 'I know how close you two were.'

Cassie felt a small but vicious twist of guilt. 'Yeah, I miss her,' she said truthfully, and added, 'I'm sure I haven't seen the last of her, though.'

'I'm *certain* you haven't. She's so fond of you. I know there was all that – trouble – last term.' Alice swallowed. 'But she's really loyal.'

'I know.' Cassie smiled back, wishing she didn't have to lie, even by omission. 'She'll be in touch soon, I'm sure.'

'Well, you'll let me know all her news when you get it, won't you?'

For the first time, Cassie felt real warmth towards her.

So Alice could be genuinely nice; who knew? She shouldn't have been surprised, really. After all, Isabella had turned to the English girl last term, when she and Cassie had fallen out so horribly over all the business with Jake and the mysterious Few deaths. All that confusion felt like a lifetime ago. But Cassie knew it wouldn't have been like Isabella to choose a complete villain or an idiot to room with when she'd temporarily moved out of their shared accommodation. Alice was a bit shallow and not that sharp, but she was a good person, Cassie thought with a stab of remorse. And she hadn't even brought up Cassie's contribution to the death of her former roommate Keiko . . .

Still, the easy companionship without the extreme closeness made her long even more to see Isabella. The class were scheduled to go out on a dusk game drive later, and Cassie found herself impatient to get it over with. Crazy to think that way about her first *game drive*, thought Cassie wryly. If she didn't have so many distractions whirling around her head, she might have been able to be more excited about it.

But by the time their Land Rover was bumping over red dust tracks, she was positively ashamed of herself. The hazy sunset turned the horizon lilac and gold, outlining thorn trees and grazing herds of gazelle and zebra. Cassie took a breath. Somewhere inside her Cranlake Crescent-self, she'd believed this stuff only existed on television. Yet there, only a few metres away, a giraffe cropped leaves from a tall tree. A *real* giraffe. She almost forgot the camera clutched in her hand, but then she began enthusiastically taking shots.

'While you're all acting like paparazzi, kindly do not forget your projects,' Professor Newham announced sternly. 'We're researching the mutual dependence between the human population and the wildlife, the contribution of tourism to sustainable development.'

'Of course we are, sir,' Richard told the geography master, po-faced. 'Nothing else ever entered my head. Well now, *that's* certainly worth documenting, for example.'

Ayeesha and Cassie spluttered as he pointed at a buffalo cumbersomely mounting another. Professor Newham glared until they recovered their composure.

'They all look so placid, considering they're some of the most dangerous animals in Africa,' murmured Ayeesha, then she turned, exclaiming, 'Oh my God, *lions*!'

It was just as well the pride was plainly used to tourists, thought Cassie; otherwise they'd have been off like a shot at the commotion on the Land Rover as they all cried out and turned to look. Still, their driver knew exactly what he was doing, following at a respectful distance but keeping in clear sight. Fascinated, Cassie watched the sleek movement of tawny muscle through the savannah grass. 'If we're lucky, we'll see a kill!' Even Professor Newham was excited.

As it turned out, they witnessed a stalk and a hunt, but the zebras got lucky – somewhat to Ayeesha's relief, Cassie realised with amusement.

'I'm just glad they didn't get that baby,' declared the Bajan girl as they finally drove back towards the camp.

'Bit tough on the poor lions,' laughed Cassie. 'They've got to eat too!'

'You could go out and help them,' said Richard, snapping his teeth and growling. 'They looked like they could use a professional.'

Cassie slapped his shoulder hard.

'Pity about the leopard no-show,' mused Newham, who seemed to have forgotten all about sustainable development.

'He's a tricky cat,' the driver called back. 'Maybe another night and a later hour, but he's very, very reticent. I wouldn't bank on seeing him at all.'

'It's OK,' said Richard. 'Cassie can go out and flirt with him and— *Ow!*'

Cassie laughed. She'd enjoyed the game drive more

than she'd have believed possible, and she was almost tempted to stay with her Few friends later that evening when they gathered round the open fire – for what Richard called 'cocktail hour', as he surreptitiously pocketed a hipflask – but the opposing attraction was too strong. Making her excuses, she slipped away into the dusk.

They'd been warned not to leave camp alone, but that rule, thought Cassie – slightly ashamed of her arrogance – could hardly be said to apply to someone with her powers. She could look after herself, no matter what came out of the night. Besides, she had to go alone and unnoticed, to get as quickly as she could to her secret rendezvous . . .

The lodge wasn't far away anyway; Sir Alric had explained where it was, a little over a mile from the camp, and she'd made a note of its position as they drove from the airstrip. The quickest route was on animal tracks through thorny scrub – *animal tracks*, she reminded herself with amusement; what absurd risks she could take as a member of the Few.

Quite. You won't be able to do THIS sort of thing if you throw me out!

'Oh, put a sock in it, Estelle.'

Apart from anything else, she wanted to enjoy the

night sounds of the bush – the cry of night birds, the low grunting of some unseen carnivore, the whistle and chirrup of cicadas. The Kenyan night wasn't exactly silent, she smiled to herself, but it was an amazing kind of racket. Eyes glinted in the brush ahead of her as she flashed her torch, but just as quickly retreated, and whatever they belonged to scurried into the undergrowth. Ahead, she could see the lights of Sir Alric's lodge now, glowing golden and welcoming from windows and veranda.

She almost ran up the steps, and they must have heard her approach. Before she could even knock on the door, it was flung open, and Isabella was hugging her, squealing with excitement.

'I missed you! *We* missed you, Cassie! It's so good to see you! Come in, come in!' Then Isabella was dragging her into the spacious interior and allowing Jake just a quick hug before shoving Cassie into a comfortable leather sofa draped with woven throws.

'Do you want a drink? You didn't *walk* all the way here, did you?' She poured Cassie a huge glass of Coke.

'Course I walked!' Cassie laughed, grinning at Jake. 'It's not that far!'

'Well, you should still be careful.' Jake shook his head, but he was smiling too.

Cassie realised again how much quieter he was now,

how much more thoughtful. Clearly a near-death experience had given him cause to reassess an awful lot.

Any gossip Cassie could provide them covered only the last few days, but Isabella was as hungry for it as Cassie was for the feeding they swiftly got out of the way. She was grateful once more for Jake's *volte-face* regarding her feeding on his girlfriend.

Jake, of course, knew little or nothing about what had happened lately at the school either, so by the time they'd relaxed after the feeding session, and Cassie was on her third Coke and finally beginning to run dry of stories, she was surprised by how many hours had passed.

She glanced at her watch. 'Whoa. I'd better get back soon. It'd be really embarrassing if they *did* send out a search party,' she said with a laugh. 'And we don't want anyone spotting you two.'

'I suppose,' agreed Isabella regretfully. 'Oh, you'll have to come back again tomorrow, Cassie. This is like old times!'

Yes, Cassie thought happily. Yes, it really was.

'I will,' she said. 'It was easy enough to get away unnoticed tonight. It shouldn't be a problem. God, it's so good to see you both!'

'One for the road?' Jake tilted an eyebrow, grinning, as he proffered the plate of brownies that she'd already overindulged in. 'Sir Alric knows a good chef when he employs one!'

'I swear I couldn't eat another bite.' Cassie patted her stomach happily, then leaned forward, biting her lip. 'I do have something to tell you both, though.'

There didn't seem a better moment, after all. Jake and Isabella quietened, watching her expectantly.

'I've got news. I think you'll like it,' Cassie continued.

'Go on.' Isabella's eyes were alight with curiosity.

Cassie took a breath. 'I'm going to split from Estelle.'

Isabella and Jake could only stare at her for a moment, then at each other.

'You what?' said Jake. 'But . . . how?'

'I've found out how to do it. That's . . . that's what all that business with Ranjit was about, last term. He'd found out how it could be done, with the Few artefacts.'

They were unexpectedly shocked and silent. Cassie raised her eyebrows.

'But look what happened to Ranjit,' said Jake quietly. 'Cassie, isn't it dangerous?'

'That was different.' She flapped a hand dismissively. 'I told you, the Curse is spent. And that was what affected him – not the Pendant itself.'

'So you really do believe it's possible? And you won't get hurt?' Jake still looked concerned.

'I do. It'll be perfectly safe,' Cassie said, hoping she sounded one hundred per cent certain even if she had a tiny seed of doubt.

Isabella reached out and clasped Cassie's arm. 'But that's wonderful! Are you really sure?'

Cassie nodded. 'I'm sure. I can't do it till I have all the things I need, and that's the next problem, but . . . yes, it can be done.'

'Cassie – you know what this means to us.' Jake hugged Isabella. 'This is great news. Fantastic!'

'And what are the "things you need"?' asked Isabella eagerly. 'Can we help?'

'Not really, no. That's where it gets tricky.' Cassie made a rueful face, then stood up and paced the room in the flickering firelight. 'Tricky, but not impossible. I'm going to do it.'

'So . . . come on, spill,' said Jake. 'What is it?'

'Well . . . you remember the Urn? The one that Ranjit got away with?' Cassie smiled weakly and spread her hands. 'That's what I need. If I can lay my hands on that, Sir Alric has agreed to use the Knife and the Pendant to cut the connection between me and Estelle.'

'And you won't be Few any more?' Isabella looked awed. 'But, Cassie, the things you can do, your prospects . . . Don't you mind about all that?'

She shrugged lightly. 'Only a little. Honestly? I'll have a couple of regrets, but not many. And I want myself back. Myself and my friends, like we used to be. That's what matters most to me. And . . . and it's the only way Ranjit and I can be together. I'm OK with it. I've made my decision and it's final.'

Isabella abandoned her place by Jake to rush to Cassie's side and hug her hard. 'Cassie,' she mumbled. 'This is wonderful. But . . . do you know where Ranjit is? Have you heard anything?'

Cassie pushed Isabella's hair out of her face and hugged her back. 'Well, not yet. But I will find him,' she said determinedly.

Isabella let go and allowed Jake to get in a hug as well. 'Good luck, Cassie,' he said, squeezing her hard. 'We're here for you, you know that, right?'

'Yeah,' Cassie replied. 'Yeah, I do . . .'

CHAPTER TEN

In the wake of Cassie's news, there was no stopping Isabella from raiding Sir Alric's fridge and opening a bottle of champagne. More than ever, Cassie felt that this was the right thing to do – even if Jake had looked a little doubtful at the mention of Ranjit.

'OK, so I get that you need to find Ranjit to get the Urn,' he said after they'd made a toast. 'But are you sure he'll help you, now that he's seen his attempt to separate you and Estelle backfire? I mean, he could have changed his mind. He is Few after all, and—'

'Not another word,' Isabella said sternly, kissing him to shut him up. 'My darling, if Cassie's certain, we should be too.'

Jake respected that injunction, but Cassie knew it must worry him a bit. After all, though he knew now that Ranjit wasn't to blame for the death of his sister

Jessica, he must still mistrust him – and not without reason, after Ranjit's mad rant at the Hagia Sophia. Still, Cassie couldn't take that into account, not right now. First her Ranjit had to be found, and the Urn, then dealing with separating Estelle's spirit; she'd take her problems as they came. There was no other way.

It was later than she'd planned by the time she kissed Isabella and Jake goodbye and set off down the veranda steps. For a moment, pausing at the edge of the scrub, she wondered if she should take the proper track this time, even if the way was a little longer.

But that was silly. She shook her head. For her remaining time as a member of the Few, she still didn't have to be afraid. Why shouldn't she make the most of it?

Besides, there was that leopard the driver had mentioned. He'd told them it haunted the area round the lodge, and it was pitch dark now, perfect for its hunting time. Cassie grinned to herself. Maybe if she was careful she might spot the big cat – and up close, while she still could.

Despite the constant background noise of insects and the rustle of small creatures in the undergrowth, she found her ears acutely attuned to the night. If she'd done her research, she thought regretfully, she could probably have distinguished some of the animals and birds individually, but she'd had too much on her mind lately. She was really going to have to relax if she could, enjoy this field trip for what it offered on the surface, and put all that was to come out of her mind for the time being.

Ranjit, of course, could never be out of her mind.

Something prickled her senses, and she came to a quiet halt. Straining her senses, she heard something move that was separate from the other night noises. Something quiet and deadly: a predator. It took one to know one, Cassie thought with a slight smile.

Crouching low, she waited. The soft padding paws drew closer through the undergrowth, then froze. She stared into the tangle of branches, waiting for the moonlight to outline the creature.

And there, miraculously, it was: sleek and beautiful, its muzzle wrinkling as it caught her scent, white fangs showing. It paused halfway out of the thicket, one spotted paw raised, and stared at her.

They held one another's gazes for long seconds, neither of them blinking. Cassie's heart was racing with joy, but outwardly she didn't move a muscle. The leopard blinked slowly, and then paced on. It passed within two metres of her, then simply padded into the scrub, and disappeared.

Cassie caught the breath she hadn't realised she was holding. As long as she lived she'd be grateful, just for that moment alone. Somehow, the leopard made it all a little more worthwhile – when she was normal once more she would be able to look back on that moment of communion with a wild thing, that moment of mutual respect, and know there had been one perfect Few instant. Cassie stood still for just a few more moments as she listened to the night – and realised, with a shock of adrenalin, that another predator was stalking her.

Tensing, baring her teeth, Cassie turned a slow circle, narrowing her eyes as she gazed into the starlit shadows.

There.

She took one step towards the malevolent presence that waited for her. It was no wild creature, that much she knew – she could *feel* it. Whatever – *whoever* – was out there, their aura was one of bright intent evil . . .

And she could sense a spirit pulsing in their chest.

'Get out here,' she snarled, 'and face me.'

There was only a second of silence. Then the branches were pushed gently aside and a beautiful girl stepped forward, pale hair glittering, eyes glowing, mouth curved in a mirthless smile. Could it really be . . . ? All that marred the girl's icy loveliness was a brutal scar along one cheekbone. Cassie well remembered putting it there. Every muscle in her body tensed for a fight to the death, and her own spirit crackled within her, aching to lash at her mortal enemy.

Katerina Svensson.

'Ding-dong Bell. I've been waiting for you.'

Katerina's voice was silkily cool and insulting. Had the girl learned nothing from their previous confrontations? wondered Cassie contemptuously.

But the Swedish girl seemed relaxed, a light of disdain in her eye. She certainly didn't look as if she was about to launch an attack, thought Cassie, her skin prickling with alertness. On the contrary, Katerina looked vindictive, triumphant – almost as if she'd already fought Cassie, and won.

'What the hell are you doing here?' Cassie spat.

What *was* Katerina doing all the way out there in Kenya? Lord knows it was unlikely she was hoping to do some independent study after having been expelled from the Academy. Cassie's eyes narrowed. Whatever the reason, wasn't this the best opportunity she would ever get? She was still Few, for now. She was still ruthless, strong: stronger than Katerina. Perhaps she could just deal with the girl here, now, once and for all . . .

Katerina smirked as if reading her thoughts. 'I suggest

you hear me out before you try anything rash.'

'You've been waiting for *me*?' Cassie made her voice as cool and disdainful as Katerina's. 'And why would you do something so reckless?'

'Aren't we the cocky little Few girl these days!' Katerina giggled viciously. 'Getting to be quite the prima donna.'

Cassie stayed silent. She wouldn't let the bitch provoke her.

Katerina prowled a circle around her, eyeing her up and down. 'Let's not indulge in any undignified scrapping, Scholarship Girl. That would be so counter-productive. After all, you are going to bring me something I want.'

Cassie turned, never taking her eyes off Katerina. 'And what's that?'

'Two things, in fact. A Knife. And a Pendant.'

Cassie gave a bark of surprised laughter. 'Even if I had them – which I don't – what makes you think it's Christmas in the Svensson household?'

'It's Christmas and my birthday rolled into one,' Katerina snarled. 'I'm going to do a deal with you, Bell.'

'I don't think so. You've got nothing I want.'

'Oh, but I *do*! That's what's so marvellous!' Katerina came to a halt, her lips peeled back in a manic smile. 'It's an offer you haven't a chance of refusing!'

Cassie watched her, breathing hard.

'Oh, Little Miss Bell! What *wouldn't* you pay for Ranjit Singh?'

CHAPTER ELEVEN

'*What?*'

'You heard me. Unless those Few senses are malfunctioning.' Katerina sniggered. 'Just two measly old antiques, and you can have Ranjit Singh.'

Cassie thought furiously. What could the insane harpy be on about? And yet she couldn't simply walk away, not now . . . could she?

'This is your best stunt ever, Katerina.' She grinned mirthlessly. 'But it ain't going to work. See you.'

She turned on her heel, hearing with some satisfaction Katerina's indrawn breath of disbelief.

'You'd be making a big mistake, Cassandra.'

Maybe it was the use of her full proper name instead of *Scholarship Girl*; maybe it was the note of malevolence in Katerina's voice. Cassie halted.

'Go on.'

'I don't need to.'

Something was flung at her feet, hitting her ankles so that she almost jumped. Slowly, filled with dread, Cassie turned and looked down. It was a lumpen thing, a shapeless tangle of canvas and straps in the dim starlight, but she knew what it was straight away.

Crouching, she picked it up by one of its straps. The backpack was empty, of course. Cassie stood straight and balanced it in her hands. It felt terrifyingly light without its last contents. Spattered across it were dark ugly stains that made her skin crawl with dread.

'Recognise that?' snapped Katerina.

'Yes,' said Cassie, trying to keep her voice flat. 'It's Ranjit's. So what?'

'Indeed it is Ranjit's. We took it from him, my mother and I. Do you see the bloodstains?'

She was trying not to. Touching the dark patches, she felt her fingertips tingle.

Yes . . . oh yes, Cassandra . . . it's his . . .

I know, Estelle. I know.

Hatred and terrible fear washed through her in a swamping tide. Cassie snapped her head up to laser Katerina with her eyes. *'Where did you get it?'*

'Ha! Mother said I'd need some other proof, but I know how your spirits are connected.'

'I know it's his blood, and you'll pay for every drop of it,' snarled Cassie. 'But what makes you think I'll give you anything? You haven't even shown me he's alive!'

'Oh, come on, Cassie,' sneered Katerina, folding her arms disdainfully. 'If he was dead you'd know it. Deep down, that spirit of yours would feel it. You have been told the history of your spirits, haven't you?' Her eyes brightened with malice and delight. 'Or perhaps not, you ignorant Scholarship! I daresay Sir Alric couldn't be bothered, for all his sentimental attachment to you. You're more of a pet to him than a student.'

Don't rise to it, Cassie told herself. That's what she wants.

'I know how desperate you are to find him,' continued Katerina. 'Aren't you, *darpak_mumbai*?' She laughed cruelly.

Cassie's legs were suddenly like rubber beneath her. *Don't show weakness! Don't!* But her voice was almost a croak when she managed to spit, 'What did you say?'

'And you can call me Tiger_eye.' The girl's lips stretched in a smirk. 'How obvious you made yourself! How we laughed, Mother and I, when we realised it was you in those chatrooms! Oh, you sad little stalker. You were so easy to deceive! You really thought it was him! You really thought it was lover-boy!'

'Why?' rasped Cassie. 'Why would you do that? If you wanted to contact me, there were much easier ways of doing it.'

'Why do you think, Scholarship?' hissed Katerina. *'For fun!'*

'Bitch,' Cassie snarled. She felt sick to her stomach.

'And, of course, to be certain that you were indeed still desperately seeking our dark hero. I mean, who knows, you may have moved on with that pathetic *snake* Richard Halton-Jones for all we knew. Fickle, us girls, aren't we—'

Katerina broke off as Cassie started towards her, her eyes glowing red.

'Uh uh uh, Cassandra. If you touch one hair on my head, you can guarantee you'll never see your precious Ranjit again. Well, certainly not with all his limbs attached . . .'

Cassie let out a growl of frustration, but backed off.

'That's better. Watch your phone, Scholarship,' said Katerina silkily. 'We'll message you when we're ready to meet, with a time and a place. Just get the artefacts we want, because we'll expect you to come as soon as we call. You have twenty-four hours from when you return to the Academy to get your clammy little paws on those artefacts. You will break into Darke's office that night and use your freaky little powers to get what we want. Do you understand?'

'And if I can't?'

'No negotiation. *Twenty-four hours*, or you'll never see him again.'

Despair swamped Cassie. She knew it was true. 'How will you know where to call me?'

Katerina giggled. 'We have your number.'

But of course they did. They had Ranjit's phone. Cassie gritted her teeth and said nothing.

'Get the artefacts. You'll be heading to Malindi. That's all you need to know for now. We'll contact you. Soon.'

Fear and a raging curiosity were almost consuming Cassie. She wouldn't ask Katerina another damn thing – not if it killed her – and besides, Ranjit *was* alive. That much she was sure of; Katerina was right. If he was dead, she'd have felt it in her soul. She had no choice but to go along with this, until she had a chance to *think* . . .

'If you've hurt him – and I see that you have – you'll pay for it, Katerina. You and your mother.'

'Oh, I'm shaking in my Choos, darling!' Katerina squeaked mockingly. 'Oh, don't hurt me, don't hurt me!'

Cassie gritted her teeth.

'Lover-boy isn't dead.' Katerina smirked. 'But fail to bring me what I want – what we want – and you'll feel him die, all right.'

135

* * *

Cassie felt numb as she blundered through thorny scrub back towards the camp. It was just as well animals seemed to be able to sense her spirit, and kept well clear, because she neither looked nor listened for danger. All she could do was hug the backpack against her body, fighting tears as she tried to think.

Come *on*, Cassie. What should she do now? What *could* she do?

Pale light was beginning to filter into the sky, and she stopped at the edge of the bush, breathless, to watch the African dawn gild the horizon. The night sounds were dying fast, replaced by morning birdsong and the grunts and movements of diurnal creatures, the rustle of gazelle and zebra cropping grass. God, it was morning already.

But it didn't matter. Cassie knew she wouldn't sleep now, anyway.

Ranjit was close; so close she felt she could almost reach out and touch him. He was there for her to take – except that in return she must hand over the very artefacts she needed if they were ever to be together.

And she knew in her bones, let alone her spirit, that Katerina and Brigitte must not get hold of the Knife and the Pendant. They already had the Urn, because they had Ranjit. She had absolutely no idea what they wanted

136

with all those ancient artefacts, but it couldn't be anything good. How could she cheerfully hand over the two powerful weapons to such an evil pair? And where was her guarantee that they wouldn't simply take the artefacts and then kill Ranjit before her eyes?

On the other hand, they'd be quite certain to kill him if she *didn't* cooperate. She couldn't kid herself about that.

She simply had to think of something else.

One thing was clear: she had to get hold of the Knife and the Pendant. She didn't want to give them to the serpentine Svenssons, but she couldn't think of any way around that at the moment.

So she was going to have to steal the artefacts. The thought made her feel sick to her stomach: she'd have to steal them from right under Sir Alric's nose. Guilt and nerves at the thought made her even more nauseous. Get over it, Cassie, she told herself. It's got to be done.

As she walked into the clearing, she stared bleakly at the Academy camp. No one was even stirring yet in the pale morning, thank God.

Something occurred to her as she stood contemplating. At least with the Knife and the Pendant in her possession, she'd be easily stronger than Brigitte and Katerina put together. She could probably defeat them without the artefacts, let alone with them – Cassie was more than a match for those women, and she'd proved it in New York when she beat hell out of them while she rescued Isabella and Jake.

With my help, dear!

Shut up, Estelle, she thought testily.

So all Cassie had to do was take the artefacts to them, rescue Ranjit, overcome the Svenssons and steal the artefacts back, go home and return them to Sir Alric, and then go through with her plan to separate from Estelle . . .

Piece of cake, right?

The very thought made her feel sick again.

Cassie made her way to her tent, hoping she hadn't been missed by Alice. She needed a bath in that ridiculously luxurious tub in the middle of nowhere first thing when the camp stirred to life. Then, she'd get down to the task in hand.

Katerina be damned; Sir Alric be damned. She was *not* leaving Ranjit to his fate.

CHAPTER TWELVE

Monday took forever to come.

She didn't have to worry that the clock was already ticking; her twenty-four hours would only start when they drove back through the gates of the Academy.

The trouble was, the twenty-four hours were already running in her head, even before they headed back to the plane. Alice noticed her distraction, the fact that she couldn't eat and didn't sleep, despite Cassie's attempts to brush her off.

None of her classmates' concern was any use to her, though, and for once it couldn't even make her feel better. Cassie could only watch the second hand crawl around her watch, the sun make its achingly slow way across the splendid Kenyan sky. When Monday morning dawned at last, she ignored all the warden's warnings about crocodiles and hippos and ran down to the river to plunge in. Just for a few seconds, she could feel light, she could wash the gnawing anxiety of what she needed to do when she got back to the Academy out of her head.

Sadly, she couldn't stay under forever.

'Cassie, you missed breakfast *again*,' said Ayeesha as she wandered back into the camp.

'I'll be glad when we get her back to the Academy,' said Cormac, hauling his backpack on to their transport with a grin. 'I reckon it could be us being surrounded by so many of our four-legged friends that's putting you off a bit of steak!'

'And sleeping in a tent isn't ideal either, no matter how fancy,' put in Alice, yawning as she emerged from their tent with her bags. Richard said nothing, just eyed Cassie suspiciously as she threw her kit together. Casually he leaned against a Land Rover, arms folded.

'Come on, Cassandra. What's up with you? You haven't been the same since the first night.'

'Nothing. Honestly. I'm just . . . looking forward to getting back.' She zipped up her backpack.

'Liar.' He lowered his voice. 'You're up to something. Spill.'

She shook her head.

'All right, be mysterious. Just take care. All right?'

Glancing up, she met his eyes, full of concern – and something more. She wished she *could* confide in him. Part of her wanted to howl and weep and ask him to sort everything out – and God knew that wasn't like her. If nothing else, she wanted him to tell her she was doing the right thing, that she wasn't making the biggest mistake of her entire life.

She trusted Richard more than anyone except Isabella – but still. This was something she had to manage alone.

'Sorry. I'm just a bit preoccupied.' Her gut twisted even more at the expression of hurt in his eyes. He knew she was holding back from him.

Just don't ask any more . . . just don't ask.

'All right.' He shrugged. 'But you know what? When you need me, I'm here. And I always will be. OK?'

It took everything Cassie had to muster up a grin for him, hoping it might help Richard not to worry.

'I know you will. I appreciate it.' She paused, biting her lip. 'And it's the same vice versa, yeah?'

And *that* at least, she thought with relief, was completely true.

One of these days, thought Cassie nervously, I am going to become someone who doesn't skulk. I will become a normal person, a person who doesn't pick locks and spy and thieve in the middle of the night. One day soon, hopefully . . .

The corridors of the Darke Academy were very quiet, except for the constant background sounds of cicadas and frogs. She almost resented those – silence suited her better, because she couldn't quite shake the feeling that the night creatures might drown out other sounds, sounds that might indicate someone was on to her. And they reminded her of the night this crazy ultimatum was put to her in the first place.

Still, it had to be done, and quickly. Even with the distraction of her secret night jaunts to visit Isabella and Jake, the four-day field trip had seemed to last an eternity; she couldn't even enjoy their company. That was partly because she hadn't felt she could confide her plans in them – not yet – and the knowledge of what she had to do back at the Academy had overshadowed everything else, simmering away in her brain till she thought it would explode.

And Estelle, of course, was no help at all.

It's a bad idea, Cassandra. A very bad idea.

Shut up, Estelle. I can hardly concentrate as it is.

Down on one knee at the door to Sir Alric's study, Cassie put her ear to the wood. All was silence and stillness. The shiny new replacement lock didn't look as if it would be a problem at all, but she still felt sick at the thought of what she was about to do – maybe even finishing off what whoever had tried it first had started . . .

And so you should! Disobedient, traitorous child! After all he's done for you.

Cassie ignored the spirit, closing her eyes and focusing on the inner workings of the lock. She felt her eyes redden as the power swelled, but despite her misgivings, she was calm and in control as she manipulated the mechanism. It gave way with a sudden click that made her catch her breath.

Cassie pushed the door gently open with one finger, creeping silently inside and closing it behind her. Pausing to glance around, she let her eyes focus in the darkness. Most likely, given Sir Alric's fondness for the familiar in some respects, the safe was in a similar position to the one in the Istanbul office. And sure enough, it took her only a few seconds to sense it there, hidden behind a row of book spines. Her fingertips tingled as she stroked them.

Lifting the books carefully down, she reached into the dark space and felt the heavy door of the safe. Now her skin was prickling with the nearness of the artefacts; she could almost hear the Knife calling to her. It had always held such a strong attraction for her, that beautiful weapon with its twisting, living carvings. She ached to touch it again, and not just because she had to steal it.

That Knife. That evil thing! It will be the death of us, Cassandra.

Estelle's voice was quiet, vicious, controlled. It wasn't like her; Cassie felt a growing sense of unease as she concentrated on projecting her strange, unique power out in front of her once more. The red point of power coalesced before her into a glowing orb . . .

And exploded. The force of it flung Cassie back. She collided with the low table and tumbled backwards with a crash.

It was shock more than pain that left her reeling. Stumbling to her feet, she shook her head violently.

'Estelle? *Estelle!* Let me do this!'

The voice was a triumphant hiss in her head. *That Knife is not for us, Cassandra!*

'Oh yes, it is, you obnoxious—' Cassie concentrated once again and directed the power back at the safe, but once more it ricocheted, scattering a rain of ornaments and pens and books that struck Cassie's head and body.

'Why, you—' Cassie gritted her teeth, clenched her fists.

No!

'Yes!'

This kind of power will not even be within your reach for much longer if you have your way! You stupid girl!

Wrestling her mind back to the safe, Cassie gripped the edge of the bookshelves and fought the obstructive spirit, her head and chest ripped with the pain of trying to wrest control. It took all her strength, and she was only vaguely aware of the crash and shatter of objects around the office as the two of them duelled. A heavy book thudded on to her toe, and Cassie yelped with anger.

'Stop it!' she barked, and with a final violent thrust, she hurled her power at the safe door. With a shriek of metal it shuddered, rattled, and swung open.

In the sudden silence, Cassie stood panting for breath, her head still throbbing.

'You old bitch,' she growled. 'What was all that for?'

You know very well. I had to try. You are DOOMING US BOTH.

With an acute awareness of the amount of noise they'd been making, Cassie hurriedly scooped the Knife and the Pendant, wrapped in soft velvet, from the safe. Even through the layers of fine fabric she felt the hilt of the Knife stir, stretch, move to her touch, and she couldn't help smiling tightly.

But there was no time to be lost. She had to try to set things to rights in this office before—

Oh, God.

The footsteps echoed at some distance along the corridor, but there was no doubt they were coming her way. It had to be Marat, surely; no one else would be around this part of the school at this hour? There was no way he'd fail to check on Sir Alric's study; no way he'd miss the chaos, especially after what had happened at the beginning of term. There was no time to do anything but hide.

Desperately, Cassie glanced around. There was nowhere to go – nowhere but the very unsatisfactory space beneath Sir Alric's desk, shielded from the rest of the room only by a delicate latticed panel of wood. Taking time only to close the safe door and shove some random books back in front of it, she scrabbled behind the desk, clutching the Knife and the Pendant against her chest. She huddled stock-still, trying to control her breathing, praying not to get caught, with everything that was at stake . . .

For a hopeful instant she thought whoever it was had passed by, but that hope shattered quickly. It was Marat. He turned the office door handle, pushed it open, and walked in.

And stopped.

Cassie held her breath. Through the holes in the lattice

she could make out his stocky form: turning, eyeing the devastation and the broken objects strewn all over the floor. She couldn't see his face, but any minute now. *Any minute now* he would raise the alarm, and she'd be discovered, and it would all be over for her and Ranjit. Maybe if Marat left the room long enough to fetch Sir Alric, maybe then she could take her chance and run. But where to? She would be the first person Sir Alric would question about this catastrophe and the missing artefacts.

The stillness was agonising. Cassie risked a slight shift in her position so that she could peer up and see Marat's ugly face.

He was smiling. The bastard was *smiling*.

Cassie's heart thudded with anxiety and incomprehension. She daren't move again, so she could only watch as he moved silently around the office: picking up books, righting lamps, replacing ornaments. When he removed the books that covered the safe she almost shrieked aloud, but all he did was replace them with other books, presumably the right ones. Then he carefully lined up the others on their original shelf.

Cassie swallowed hard, fighting to control the thrashing of her heart.

Marat was checking the room over again; adjusting the position of a table slightly, straightening a chair. Casually, he tilted a glass lampshade to a lower angle, and brushed a broken piece of porcelain into his hand and then his pocket. He smiled once more, his face a picture of satisfaction.

And then, very quietly, he left the office, and closed the door behind him.

CHAPTER THIRTEEN

What the hell was that? Cassie crawled out from under the desk and shook her head, looking around the now-tidy office. But she didn't really have time to fret about Marat's odd behaviour. Because of it, there was a good chance Sir Alric wouldn't realise for a little while that he'd been burgled, but that breathing space wouldn't last for long. She had to get out of there, and get north as fast as possible.

The Academy was in darkness and silence as the night pressed on. Cassie wished that there were more than half of her twenty-four hours left, but it couldn't be helped. Her heart pounded as she ran silently through the school grounds and out to the road.

There was very little traffic at first and she had to walk some distance, but as the sky lightened the roads grew rapidly busier, and she could flag down a succession of rickety *matatus* that took her north towards Mombasa, the artefacts now tucked inside Ranjit's bloodstained backpack. From her now-solitary room, she'd grabbed a few thousand Kenyan shillings (rather a lot of them Isabella's, she remembered guiltily), along with her passport and smartphone.

Look on the bright side, she told herself, glancing at her watch. She had as good a head start as she could possibly expect. This latest brightly coloured *matatu* was full at six in the morning, but it made pretty good speed up the coastal road – sometimes too good, she thought, glad they'd made the drivers fit seatbelts as she was thrown against hers for the umpteenth time. She still hugged the backpack tightly against her body; it might make it look more valuable and worth stealing, but let anyone try. She wasn't letting it out of her sight or touch.

It would all be over soon. She'd have Ranjit; defeat the Svenssons; take the artefacts back to the Academy. How hard could it be?

Cassie let out a short, hysterical laugh, earning odd looks and a few comments from her fellow passengers. She was absolutely exhausted, she realised. By the time she'd changed minibus in the thronged streets of Mombasa, she had decided that, Few or not, it was really not a good idea to draw attention to herself. She curled in her seat, head against the window and huddled round the backpack, and pretended to go to sleep.

And promptly did.

When Cassie woke with a start, the sun was high and her body was sticky with sweat. Oh God, how could she have actually slept? Apart from the fact she hadn't done so for four nights . . .

For a hideous instant she imagined her arms were empty, but as she stirred, pains shooting through her limbs from stiffness and immobility, she felt the backpack clutched against her, her whole body wrapped around it. A skinny guy on the other side of the *matatu* was sitting sideways, staring at the backpack with a calculating expression, but one look at Cassie's eyes – reddened not just with sleep – and he swung round to face forward again.

Her limbs ached, and she stretched as well as she could, peering out of the window. She had to be close to Malindi now, and far north of Mombasa; wasn't that what the message had said? Even as she reached for her phone she felt it suddenly vibrate in her pocket, and she snatched it out, peering desperately at the screen.

Ranjit Singh

Even though she knew it wasn't really him, only his

stolen property, her heart gave a lurch of sickening hope. Cassie thumbed the screen desperately to read the message.

Gedi ruins. Driver will stop.

Cassie glared around, eyeing her fellow passengers – the potential mugger now looking downright nervous – and shading her eyes to gaze at the road and countryside beyond the rickety bus. There was no one she could detect who might be tracking her for the Svenssons, and she hated the very idea, but one of them must be. The thought that her enemy knew her movements, yet she could not see them, made the hairs rise on the back of her neck. The driver showed no sign of either watching her, or slowing the *matatu*'s hectic pace.

She sighed. Gedi ruins? Tapping open the internet browser on her phone, she scrolled down the search results.

Gedi: the ruins of a fifteenth-century Arab-African town on the Mombasa–Malindi road, ten miles south of Malindi. Founded in the late thirteenth or early fourteenth century and abandoned in the early seventeenth. Archaeological fragments indicate that it had a large and prosperous population.

So far so normal, Cassie thought with a roll of her eyes. There was nothing the Few liked better, for an assignation, than a pile of old ruins. God forbid they should ever

152

arrange a showdown in a nice clean shopping centre.

Idly she tapped a link and opened another website. There wasn't much.

In the sixteenth century, an unexplained occurrence brought the life of Gedi to a temporary end.

Cassie frowned. Curiouser and curiouser, she thought. Unexplained occurrences were another of the Few's favourite things . . .

For what felt like the hundredth time, she was jolted against her seatbelt as the *matatu* swerved to an abrupt halt. Cassie looked up sharply. The driver's eyes met hers in his cracked rear-view mirror.

There didn't seem any need to ask if this was her stop. Grabbing the backpack, pocketing her phone, she felt the eyes of every passenger follow her as she swung down out of the *matatu*. The driver gave her one more look, entirely expressionless.

She didn't wave. He gunned the rickety vehicle into life and roared away in a cloud of red dust.

Cassie stared after it, her stomach like lead. She'd half-expected – half-hoped for – tourists, crowds of them; and yet why would she imagine such a thing? It wouldn't suit the Svenssons to have people around, and besides, they'd want to unnerve her, to make her feel wholly alone. That certainly wouldn't be such a terribly difficult thing to arrange, in this deserted site where only dust and ghosts seemed to move among the stones.

Face it, Cassie: you haven't a clue what you're going to do about all of this. She shut her eyes, allowing the fear and apprehension to wash over her like a gigantic wave, just for a moment.

No! No time for that. Cassie swallowed hard. Hoisting the backpack on to her shoulder, she walked silently towards the empty ticket office and beyond it into the ruins. In the empty vastness, the air felt ancient and heavy around her, thick with spirits.

Not too many of my kind, I hope, she thought with a shiver.

Cassie stepped through an arched doorway into a roofless courtyard, her heart banging her ribs. Many of the walls were worn down to their foundations by the centuries, but the outline of a town lay there like a skeleton, or perhaps a ghost. At the flap of wings she looked up, startled, and saw a dusty-looking buzzard watching her. Trees grew where people must once have lived and worked and laughed, their branches overhanging the old rooms; an eerie sensation skittered down Cassie's spine with a frisson of familiarity.

She'd never been anywhere like this, she was sure of it, but there was something haunting the edges of her memory. Then she realised: Angkor Wat.

She hadn't ever actually been in the Cambodian temple ruins where Jake's sister Jessica had died. But she felt as if she had, and she was certain that the place where Keiko had discovered the Knife must have this same sense of ancient ruins only sleeping. Only sleeping, but still breathing, still living.

Cassie shook herself. There was no sign of modern life, that was for sure, but she knew it was here somewhere. They were here somewhere . . . and that meant he was too. The knowledge of Ranjit's nearness gave her a surge of hope, but she couldn't be complacent. She had to stay alert.

Still nothing moved but trees and birds and insects, and a snake that slithered quickly into the undergrowth as she walked carefully on. Where the hell were they? The sun blazed down on her unprotected head; wishing belatedly that she'd remembered to bring a hat, she stood in the shade of an archway and thumbed the screen of her phone once more. It was more to pass the time than out of genuine curiosity, but a paragraph caught her eye. She scrolled quickly back up to it.

Earthenware pots with a magical purpose have been found buried at several points throughout the ruins. A charm would be placed in the pot by the homeowner which, together with special rituals, enticed a djinn to enter them. This guardian spirit, should anyone enter the house with evil intent, would drive the thief mad.

Cassie's throat felt suddenly very dry. No, she thought. Don't be silly. That's old superstition, no more. The Svenssons had doubtless brought her here knowing how unnerving the place was – and how conveniently abandoned.

All the same, she wished they'd hurry up and show their hand. The sun was beginning to dip back towards the horizon, and Few or not, she did not want to be here in the dark, with djinns and ghosts and who knew what else . . .

Cassie's fingers tightened on the backpack strap. *Come on.* She was being foolish, not to mention cowardly. She couldn't let any fear cloud her mind, or she'd never pull this off. Of course she wouldn't simply hand the Knife and the Pendant to those two evil bitches. She'd beaten them before, and with ease; and she was more confident in her power now than she had been, even in New York when she'd given them such a thrashing. True, she had no particular plan, but she'd play it by ear. When she left this place – and she'd be more than happy when that moment came – she'd have Ranjit and the artefacts. The Svenssons, damn their icy eyes, would have nothing.

It wasn't as if she thought for a moment that they'd hand Ranjit over. More than likely the Svenssons were planning their own double-cross, and intended to kill them both. Cassie was not going to let that happen.

She jumped as the phone in her hand vibrated again.

Ranjit Singh

Angry with herself for the leaping of her heart, Cassie tapped the message.

The Palace. Turn right. Then 40 metres.

Cassie swallowed, assailed again by that horrible sense of being watched. But at least it was time to move and to act. She didn't know how much longer she could have stood it, waiting in the eerie silence of the ruined town.

The shadows of the crumbling walls seemed to grow longer as she walked the last few metres and climbed ramshackle steps. Throat tight and blood pounding, she stepped through a pointed archway and made her way silently through the roofless rooms. The walls were pocked with holes where lamps must have once burned, but there were none now, of course: only the shifting low sunlight and the unnerving shadows.

At the entrance to a smaller chamber Cassie stopped, listening. Now. She was sure.

As if waiting only for her thought, the two women stepped out into the gathering twilight: Katerina and

Brigitte Svensson, palely beautiful and haughty. And triumphant, thought Cassie bitterly.

And there, between them, sagging in their grip, they held the wounded Ranjit Singh.

Cassie couldn't help sucking in a lungful of air. For an instant she felt dizzy, but she got a grip on herself fast, gripping the backpack strap so hard her fingernails dug painfully into her palms.

Ranjit wasn't looking at her. His head drooped forward, and when Katerina seized his hair and yanked it up, Cassie wanted to be sick, and her heart choked her throat. His face was bruised and bloody, but that wasn't the worst of it; the worst was his eyes, which had the stunned, unseeing glaze of the deeply drugged. She had to restrain herself from crying out, dropping everything and rushing over to him.

Gritting her teeth, Cassie stepped up to meet her enemies, swinging the backpack carefully down from her shoulder.

'Give him to me,' she growled.

'Give us the artefacts,' snarled Brigitte.

Immobilised by indecision, Cassie looked for the first time beyond the two women. No, she hadn't imagined it: there was a light, glowing softly in an alcove behind them, but growing more intense as she watched. There was something about that light she didn't like one bit. Cassie frowned, and met Katerina's eyes.

'Give me Ranjit. That was the deal. Wasn't it, Tiger_eye?'

Katerina shook her captive's arm roughly, smirking at Cassie, her eyes red with spirit-light and fury.

'Hah! Come on then, Scholarship. Come on and take him!'

CHAPTER FOURTEEN

Cassie stepped forward. Never letting her gaze leave Katerina's face, she reached into the backpack. As she closed her fingers round the hilt of the Knife, she felt its carvings stir into life, and the old inevitable thrill ran through her veins.

'Show me,' hissed Katerina.

Cassie drew out the Knife and the Pendant in one hand. The light that seeped from the alcove behind the Svenssons made the artefacts gleam with a supernatural light.

Brigitte's eyes were brilliant with greed. 'Now hand them over.'

Cassie slipped the artefacts back into the backpack, letting go of the Pendant but keeping her fingers lightly around the Knife's hilt in the confines of the bag. She stretched the backpack towards Katerina. As the blonde girl reached for the straps, Cassie shut her eyes once, then snapped them open. She flung the backpack aside, the Knife still clutched in her hand.

As she'd hoped, Katerina and Brigitte lunged for the backpack before they'd realised what Cassie was doing. She took her chance to leap for Ranjit as they let him fall.

Cassie seized Ranjit, catching him in her arms and staggering backwards. Just feeling him against her gave her renewed strength. Keeping one arm protectively around him, she raised the Knife, her teeth gritted.

Brigitte saw what had happened first, and spun round with a snarl.

But Cassie realised she couldn't protect Ranjit and keep her eyes on them both. Katerina's blow came from her blind side, knocking her back against the wall and stunning stars into her vision. She scrambled up, just in time to feel Brigitte's boot connect with her ribcage, kicking her back down. The Knife spun from her grip.

No! This couldn't happen! Summoning every last scrap of the power inside her, Cassie felt her eyes burn red as she stood over Ranjit, snarling and lashing out with her projected spirit. She put everything into it, striking out viciously at the two women.

They reeled, raising their arms to shield themselves by reflex, but they didn't fall. They barely tottered. Cassie screamed with frustration as their joint power flung her back yet again, so that she stumbled over Ranjit's prone body and fell. Brigitte flew for the Knife, reaching it before Cassie had even got back on her feet.

God, she had to think of something! Feeling blood trickle into her eyes, Cassie wiped it furiously away with a fist as she gasped for breath. Beyond Brigitte and Katerina, that weird light was now intense, roiling and pulsing, and in a hideous instant Cassie recognised its shape. It was the Urn – the Urn—

The women were using it somehow, drawing strength from it. Its light seemed to engulf Brigitte and Katerina, intensifying the spirit-light in their chests, until the two women were blindingly bright themselves. And unbeatable—

The knowledge crashed into Cassie's brain with appalling certainty. For the first time she panicked, striking violently, wildly, but the women fell on her with fists and feet, and pain seemed to explode all over her body at once.

'Kill her!' screamed Brigitte. 'Once and for all!'

Lifting her fists to strike them back, Cassie didn't even have time to project her power before she was struck to the ground again, slammed and kicked. Despair struck her at the same time, with a gut-punch force.

She had to get away, get away or die—

Through blood-blinded red vision she saw the backpack. It was within her reach, discarded on the ground as her enemies focused on the joy of giving her a thrashing, of finally doing away with her. With a grunt of desperation Cassie grabbed at the pack, her fingers closing on its strap. She didn't want to give it up – with the Pendant gone too, all would certainly be lost – but she knew, very suddenly and surely through the pain and shock, that she was out of options. She and Ranjit would die here if she didn't do this.

Cassie managed to get her legs underneath her, scramble to her feet and propel herself upright, swaying as Brigitte and Katerina came at her again. With the last of her strength, Cassie swung back the backpack and flung it hard at the glowing Urn.

'Take it!' she screamed.

A direct hit. It crashed into the Urn, knocking it backwards so that it bounced and rolled back into the next room, the backpack flying after it. Brigitte and Katerina howled as one, and turned to sprint after it. Cassie didn't waste even a fraction of a second. She stumbled to Ranjit, hauling his arm across her shoulders and half-dragging him out of the Palace ruins.

She hadn't broken the Urn; not only had she heard it

bounce and roll, she didn't believe for a moment that victory would be so easy. But she must have put the fear of God into Katerina and Brigitte, because they didn't follow, too concerned with the Urn and any possible damage to it. Hauling Ranjit with her, she dragged him on, pulling him through the entrance archway desperately, expecting the women's vengeful return at any moment.

But there was no sign or sound of them. Well, why would they bother? They had all three artefacts now. They had no further use for her – they knew she was defeated. Gasping for breath, Cassie stumbled through the ruins, Ranjit a sluggish weight against her.

But I have Ranjit . . . I do have him . . .

Somehow, it didn't calm the sickening sensation of failure and horror in her gut. Oh God, Cassie, she thought, as she pulled Ranjit past the ticket office and away from the ruins. What have you done?!

She couldn't think about it, not now. All that mattered was getting Ranjit away and to safety. She didn't know how they'd drugged him, or what they'd done to him before that, but he wasn't looking good.

Her strength gave way just beyond the ruins, at the roadside. Stumbling, she let Ranjit slump against a wall. Leaning on her thighs, panting for breath, aching all over from her beating, Cassie let her breath slow and, finally, calm.

At last she allowed herself to really study the long, lean figure laid on the ground beside her. It was him. This was no dream, like the ones that had haunted her since she watched him flee from the Hagia Sophia. It was Ranjit, and he was with her, for now, no matter the circumstances.

She couldn't fight it any more – all she wanted was to feel him in her arms. Kneeling, Cassie pulled his body towards her, hugging him to her hard, caressing his blood-soaked hair, kissing his face and his eyes, feeling tears of exhaustion and relief trickle down on to his skin.

A single sob escaped; then she sat back on her heels and took his beautiful face in her hands. Stroking his cheekbones with her thumbs, she begged him inwardly.

Oh, wake up. Please wake up . . .

His dark eyelashes trembled. Leaning close, she kissed his eyes and mouth and skin.

'Wake up,' she whispered urgently. 'Oh, Ranjit. Please be OK. Please.'

His golden eyes flickered open. For long moments they were blurred, seeming to look through and past her, and then, miraculously, they focused, and something like a smile twitched the corner of his mouth.

'Ranjit?'

'Cassie . . . Cassie . . .'

'It's me,' she whispered, her voice ragged.

'Oh my God. Cassie. Wh-what happened?'

'It doesn't matter. You're all right. I've got you.'

His fingers closed around her wrists as if he wanted to make sure, to feel the strength of her pulse. 'Cassie . . .' Reaching out, he touched her face.

'It's OK, really. I'm here.'

'Oh thank God. Thank God.' He wrapped his arms round her, and she felt tears sting her eyes at the weakness of his grip.

'Ranjit . . .' She could hardly stand to make him stop. 'We have to get moving. We're not safe yet.'

'All right . . .' He looked up into her eyes, and suddenly his smile faded. The skin between his eyes creased with a terrible anxiety.

'Wait, Cassie – the artefacts . . .' But his eyelids were drooping again.

'Ranjit?'

'You mustn't let them . . .'

'Ranjit?' she said, her voice panicked.

He slumped back, limp again, his eyes closed.

Cassie stared at him, her mind in turmoil. He was breathing softly, passed out again.

She swallowed. But I have you, she thought. I have

you, Ranjit, and that's the most important thing right now. The rest, I'll deal with when I get us out of here . . .

Quite right, my dear! Don't worry about those old relics! Let's go home!

'Shut up, Estelle!' Cassie snapped. But remembering it was the spirit's cooperation that had helped her get Ranjit back, she softened slightly. 'Like you should be calling anything an old relic,' she muttered.

Such petulance, my dear! You should be thankful.

The spirit sounded brighter and bouncier than she had in a long time, Cassie thought darkly. And understandably, because without the Knife and the Pendant . . . No. She wouldn't even think about it till she got Ranjit to safety.

That, of course, was going to be a challenge, with him unconscious once more, his breath barely stirring in his lungs, and them more than seventy miles from the Academy. Tears sprang to Cassie's eyes, but she blinked them away. Ranjit was relying on her, whether he knew it or not.

Her physical strength, at least, was returning; she could feel the powerful adrenalin of desperation flowing in her blood and muscles. The spirit inside her was growing hungry after the effort of the fight and the beating she'd taken, but she had to get Ranjit away from here. Getting to her feet, Cassie hauled him up. It took three tries, but at last she got her arm securely under him and she could hoist him up with a grunt. Cassie staggered out into the road, dragging him with her.

And what are you going to do now? Walk to Mombasa?

The sun was below the horizon, and the sky was darkening fast; they mustn't be here much longer. Cassie was thinking so furiously, and with such a crushing sense of hopelessness, she barely heard the throaty rumble of a vehicle.

At last it penetrated the fog of her thoughts. It was racing towards her from the north, its engine sounding tortured, the gears grinding as it skidded round the nearest corner. Cassie had time only to drop Ranjit like a sack of potatoes, and then stumble out into the road, waving her arms wildly.

The *matatu* swerved and jolted to a stop, stalling only a couple of metres away from her. Its driver goggled at her through the dirty windscreen; it wasn't her previous *matatu* and driver, she realised with a gasp of relief – the one who had clearly been under instructions from the Svenssons. And even more to her relief, the vehicle was empty.

Before this driver could gun the ignition again, Cassie jumped on board, tugging her battered wallet from her back pocket. She flourished it at him.

'Hey! No, no. I'm going home,' he protested. 'Day's over, *mzungu*.'

'Please. Wait. I'll pay you. I'll pay you whatever you want. Private hire.'

He hesitated, looking at the notes. She was glad she'd brought so much. 'Where to?'

'Mombasa.' She hesitated. 'Well, just past Mombasa.'

He eyed her suspiciously. 'That will cost you a lot of money.'

'I don't care.' Cassie glanced back at Ranjit, slumped in the road like a corpse.

'What's wrong with him?'

'He's . . . he's very drunk. I need to get him back to school. We'll get in trouble.' Cassie took a deep breath. 'I'll pay whatever you want. Please.' She racked her brain for a useful phrase. '*Tafadhali*.'

He made a face, then looked out at the road.

'*Ndiyo*. Get your friend.'

Cassie stayed wide awake through this journey; her bones were too rattled, her brain buzzing, for any sleep now. Nor could she bear to think about the ramifications of what she'd done; all she could do was stare down at Ranjit and stroke his bruised but beautiful face. He lay across her lap, not stirring, barely breathing, his body jolting violently every time the *matatu* hit a pothole. She held him as tightly as she dared, trying to cushion his body against the wild ride. Occasionally he half-woke, and gave a groan of pain, but he always slipped back into oblivion. In some ways she was glad. Ranjit had been on the run from all of this; she doubted he'd come back to the Academy with her voluntarily.

It was the smallest, darkest hours of the tropical night when the *matatu* finally bumped to a halt at the end of the school's drive. The driver clearly couldn't wait to get back home, and Cassie was just as eager to get into the school unseen. She emptied the contents of her wallet into his hands and dragged the half-conscious Ranjit quickly from the vehicle. As she listened to the grinding engine fade and vanish into the night, she slumped on to the driveway, Ranjit in her arms.

'Come on. It'll be dawn soon,' she murmured. 'We need to get you inside.'

It still wasn't easy, but at least he was able to stumble limply down the drive and across the grass, sending a family of warthogs stampeding in fright into the bush. He clearly still wasn't aware of where they were, Cassie thought thankfully. The side door they came up to was alarmed, but after the day she'd just had, it seemed the easiest of tasks to propel her fading power into the mechanism and disable the lock. The sky outside was beginning to grey with the sunrise as she hooked her hands under Ranjit's armpits and helped him up the stairway and along the passage to her room. She opened the door, staggered inside, and helped Ranjit to lie across the bed. Closing the door behind them quietly, she sighed with a rush of relief. Good timing, she told herself as she heard the first stirrings of Academy life. If anyone had woken up a moment earlier, they'd have caught her and Ranjit. And she'd have had even more explaining to do.

Cassie bent over, catching her breath. Not for long, though. There wasn't really any time to do anything as prosaic as properly recovering. Still, she stood over Ranjit for a moment, caressing his face. So she finally had him in her bed. The circumstances could have been better, she thought wryly, as tears threatened to choke her throat.

Clenching her fists, Cassie pressed her eyes shut and controlled herself. There was no point in putting this off. She was not looking forward to explaining herself to Sir Alric, but she hadn't a choice. She'd done all she could for Ranjit; now, much as she hated to admit it, they both needed Darke's help to try and put things right.

She might as well get it over with.

CHAPTER FIFTEEN

Cassie took a deep breath and held it in her lungs for a few seconds, but there was no going back now. She sighed hard, raised her fist and knocked loudly on Sir Alric's door.

He opened it himself. 'Cassie! What on earth—'

His eyes were wide, and he seemed stunned as he looked her up and down. No wonder, she thought ruefully. What a sight she must look: bruised, bloody, coated in dust, and gaunt from spirit-hunger.

'Sir Alric.'

Darke shook himself. He reached out and took her arm, pulling her into his office and almost pushing her bodily into an armchair.

'What's happened?'

Cassie felt suddenly dizzy, and very sick. She bent her head into her hands, waiting for the tide of nausea to pass.

When she glanced up, he was holding a glass of water in one hand, and a phone in the other.

'Yes,' he was saying into it as she shakily took the water. 'My office at once, please, Miriam. No, you're not in trouble. It's just a message I was asked to pass on.'

Sir Alric hung up and turned to his desk, taking a vial from a drawer and mixing its contents into a crystal tumbler of water. 'Miss Bell, I hope you have a good explanation for all of this.'

'I have . . . an explanation,' she mumbled.

'Miriam McEwen will be here directly. You know her from your fencing classes, I believe; she's physically strong and she does not have a Few roommate at present. She's up early as she's on the rowing team, but she'll just have to miss training today. When she arrives she'll take this drink, and you will feed from her. No argument; I'm not presently interested in your moral scruples. Now, start talking. You have ten minutes.'

Cassie's stomach lurched, but she had no option. Beginning with her meeting with Katerina near the hunting lodge, she told him everything – haltingly, her voice occasionally dropping to a whisper, but she left nothing out. When she reached the part about breaking into his office the previous night, her throat dried up altogether, and she had to knock back the rest of the water before she could continue. The confession was so painful she had to pause to regain her breath; she remembered that she had to explain about Marat, too, and his odd behaviour. That would have to wait – and besides, it was the only part of the tale that didn't quite make sense. She'd let the rest sink in first.

Sir Alric had gone very still, and his face was deathly pale. Cassie's heart felt like a shrivelled thing in her chest. For long moments, she thought she was going to get away with it. She thought, very fleetingly, that he was too shocked to speak.

And then he exploded.

'I have striven for years to keep those artefacts out of the wrong hands. Years! And now you, Cassie Bell, have just handed them over.'

'I'm sorry. I . . . I had no choice. I—'

'You always have a choice! Do you have any idea what you've done? No! No, you obviously don't, because no one with even a solitary brain cell would do something so stupid. You wanted your boyfriend back, so you've handed over all us Few to get him. Every damned one of us, Cassie!'

She had never, never seen him lose his temper like this. Crushed into silence, she waited for him to yell again, to break the awful tension in the air.

He didn't. All she could hear was his furious breathing.

'What will they do?' she managed in a small voice. 'The Svenssons?'

He made an angry, despairing gesture, but when he spoke again his voice was lowered. 'I don't know. I daresay we'll find out soon enough, thanks to you.' He tightened his fists, and when she dared to meet his eyes she saw that they were misted with red. He breathed hard, calming himself. 'What do you think they wanted with the artefacts? Did they say anything? Think, girl. Think of anything that might help.'

'I don't know . . . they didn't explain.' Cassie's voice shook. 'But . . . the Urn, when it glowed – there was something about it. It seemed to . . . I don't know, give them some kind of extra power. They were drawing strength from it. The light was like . . . like a living thing.'

'Living?'

'Yes. Maybe there are still spirits trapped in it? From way back, when the Eldest fed on—'

Sir Alric held up his hands and shook his head, frowning. 'I'll do the thinking from now on, Miss Bell.' He paced the room. 'As for Ranjit Singh—'

There was a hesitant knock on the outer door that stopped him. Startled, they both glanced at it, and Sir Alric barked, 'One minute, Miriam.'

He lowered his voice, leaning menacingly over Cassie. 'All I can do is try to undo the harm you've done. Minimise it, at least. Listen to me, Miss Bell. I'll have to leave the Academy to attempt to locate the Svenssons, or at least try to determine what it is they have planned. I will go to the lodge at Mount Kenya, because that's where I stored all the related documents after that last – unsuccessful – break-in. And I take it, since it was unsuccessful, that you weren't the culprit.'

Cassie shook her head. The break-in. 'There's something I've got to—'

'I don't want any more apologies,' he interrupted bitterly. 'I had sent the documents to Mount Kenya for safekeeping. Not the artefacts, because I didn't want to let those out of my sight. I realise now that I shouldn't have been so foolish. But I didn't allow for treachery quite like this.'

Cassie couldn't speak.

Sir Alric straightened and went back to his desk drawer. He threw a key into her lap, and she caught it, eyes widening as she recognised the carved symbols.

'That, as you will remember, is the key to Jake's old room. Ranjit may as well stay there. He should take time to recuperate, since his life has been bought so dearly. Of course,' he added savagely, 'he can't even use the Tears to aid his recovery, since Jake has those at the lodge. But I daresay you will find some means to tend him, Miss Bell. And make sure no further disturbance occurs.'

Cassie nodded, keeping her lips tightly shut. She wanted so desperately to be back with Ranjit now, to remind herself why she'd done this terrible thing in the first place. She couldn't think straight any more.

'One more thing,' Sir Alric said. 'I'll help you get Mr Singh to his new quarters. But once there, you will not get involved with him in any romantic way. For once in your life you will do as you are told. There's no chance of you splitting from your spirit, now that you've given away the means to do it.' He sounded almost spiteful, and for once she didn't blame him. 'So you will keep your spirits apart. For once in your life you will consider the impact of your actions on the rest of the Few, and you will restrain your impulses. Do I make myself clear?'

'Yes,' whispered Cassie. If he didn't let up, she thought, she was going to faint, and that would be the ultimate humiliation.

He stared at her. 'And now, you're going to feed.' He strode to the door, and his voice was suddenly warm and welcoming and perfectly civil.

'Good morning, Miriam. Thank you for coming so

swiftly. Can I offer you a vitamin drink. This won't take
long at all.'

Much later, Cassie sat on the edge of a chair in what
she still thought of as Jake's quarters, gazing at the
sleeping Ranjit.

No wonder Sir Alric had let rip at her. And no wonder
he'd done it before she fed. Now, restored with poor
Miriam's unwitting help, Cassie's mind was racing
again, and she could feel the old energy trickling back, the
old defiance.

She'd deserved it; she knew that. What she'd done was
unforgivable. But it had also been unavoidable. Now she
just had to start fixing things . . .

Rising, she went over to Ranjit's bed and sat down on
the edge, stroking his hair and his face and the arm that
lay on top of the covers. It was lean and pale, but still
muscled, and the fist was clenched in his sleep.

By the time Ranjit had been brought up here, Sir Alric
was a little more his old cool self. He'd calmed down
enough to do some explaining; maybe, despite his fury,
he'd realised that explanations could still stave off disaster
more effectively than keeping secrets.

'Your spirits have always been ruthless, the pair of
them,' he'd told her as they stood looking down at Ranjit.

'Ruthless and, as you know, tremendously powerful. And always, always passionately connected. At the very heart and soul.'

'So what was so wrong with that? What happened?' By that time, she was already feeling strong enough to question him again.

'Your spirits' first incarnations were mortal dynastic enemies. They were sworn to crush one another in battle, yet their love was something that couldn't be resisted. You may imagine the diplomatic chaos that ensued. The chaos, and the carnage. Treachery, passion, conflicting loyalties, and the utter confusion of their people and their armies. The Few that originally housed your spirits learned to combine their powers, thereby multiplying them exponentially. Together they were irresistible as a force of war, but their soul-deep rivalry could no more be denied than their soul-deep love. They quarrelled, they fought, they went to war once more; and yet they could not stay away from each other. The spirits that had once combined, collided. Their empires and their armies and their nations: all were turned to dust.'

Cassie had swallowed. 'Both sides?'

'Both. And not merely once. The first time, as I seem to remember from the records, it was the host of your spirit who finally plunged a blade into the chest of her lover –

the Knife of the Few, as it happens – but you are aware how strong your spirits are. He survived long enough to escape into a new host – I believe your spirit made sure of that, by having a new young host ready and waiting – and he eventually retaliated in your next incarnations. In three different generations of spirit-birth, history repeated itself. He has murdered you almost as often as you have murdered him.'

Cassie had swallowed.

'Whenever your spirits came together, they were deadly both to other Few and to the human race. They were too alike – like an atom that had been split. Perhaps, once, they were a single spirit, divided somehow. But now they are two: forever . . . in love. And forever at war. The war part, humanity can handle, just. It's the passion behind their power that is deadliest of all.'

'What about Estelle Azzedine? The old woman, I mean, not her spirit. Why wasn't she trying to rip Ranjit's clothes off when I met her in Paris and got into all this mess?'

'She would have,' he'd told her grimly, 'if I'd allowed them to ever meet. Remember, Ranjit had been host to his spirit for only a few years by then. Before that, Estelle was the lover of his spirit's previous host.' He added, matter-of-factly, 'She killed him, of course.'

'So . . . Oh God, is that why she chose me? So that she could be close to Ranjit again?'

'It was one of many factors. It didn't escape anyone's attention that he was attracted to you even before you became Few. Well, Estelle got her way in the end as you know, despite my efforts to stop it. But believe me, this will end badly. If you fail to listen to me, that is.'

'But it's our *spirits* you're talking about here!' Cassie had blurted. 'It's not Ranjit and me who do the killing, it's them!'

'You *are* your spirits; they are you.' His eyes were cold and hard. 'There is no difference. Accept it, and we might be able to control the collateral damage. Disobey me, give in to your desire for Ranjit, and there will be carnage. Again.'

Cassie had repeated his words to herself, over and over again. She believed Sir Alric absolutely, she couldn't deny it. In this she trusted him; she remembered Katerina's taunts about the things she hadn't been told; and more vividly than that, she remembered the violent wildness that stirred and flared into fire whenever she'd touched Ranjit.

Oh, she believed Sir Alric, all right.

Obeying him? That was another matter entirely.

So their spirits must never be together. Fine, and fair

enough. But Sir Alric be damned; *she and Ranjit* could and would.

She'd blown it by giving away those artefacts, and she was even more angry with herself than Sir Alric was. But damn the Svenssons, and damn their plans. She'd find them, and get the artefacts back. Cassie clenched her jaw determinedly. She didn't care how long it took: she'd free herself from the spidery, choking clutches of the Few spirit inside her.

CHAPTER SIXTEEN

The corridors seemed alien and strange, teeming with normal school life, echoing with the shouts and chatter of students who were thinking of nothing but lunch. It all seemed to Cassie like life on a distant planet.

She wasn't even hungry herself, but she'd been determined to grab something from the dining room that might tempt Ranjit when he woke again, properly this time. It was a moment she was desperate for, but at the same time she wasn't sure how he was going to react to everything that had happened. She just hoped Ranjit would be OK. For the first time she'd found herself resenting Jake, resenting the fact that he'd had the Tears, that he'd even taken the remainder with him so that nothing was available for Ranjit.

But Jake had nearly *died*, Cassie reminded herself. And it was Ranjit who'd done that to him.

It never got any easier wondering how on earth things were going to work out for the best. Clutching a soft roll and some cheese wrapped in a linen napkin, she turned into her own corridor, worrying for the first time about the other type of hunger Ranjit would inevitably have by the time he woke up . . .

Cassie was so distracted by her thoughts that she let out an involuntary gasp as she saw a figure standing in front of her. Richard was standing at her door, hand raised as if he'd only just knocked on the door, or was about to. As she arrived he turned, and gave her a broad surprised smile.

'Cassie! There you are. Where have you been?'

She hesitated. 'It's a long story. Can it . . . ah . . . wait?'

He stepped closer, trying to catch her eye. 'Well, I'm here now,' he said. 'And you look like you could use someone to talk to?'

Cassie hesitated – if there was anyone to unload all this stress on, it was Richard.

'Come on, Cassie Bell,' Richard said with a raised eyebrow and an encouraging smile. 'You're up to something, and I want to know what it is. You weren't anywhere to be seen yesterday. You weren't at breakfast this morning, and you cut Maths. Maths! What's wrong with you, gorgeous? Are you sick?'

'As if,' she blustered. 'I'm tired, that's all. After the field trip.'

'Alice made it to Maths,' he scolded. 'And you weren't up till six on Monday morning, canoodling with Yuri in his tent. Well, not unless things got more interesting than even I had heard . . .'

'No!' Cassie gaped, drawn in despite herself. 'I wondered where she'd got to . . .'

'And now you know. Which means you owe me. Come on, seriously. Spill.'

She watched him, biting the inside of her lip. This felt like the other half of that conversation they'd started yesterday morning at Mount Kenya: the one about him always being there when she needed him. And she did trust him.

'Richard, I'm in trouble.'

'That much I guessed. Do you need a feeding source? I can always offer Perry again, he does have some uses after all . . .'

'Well, now that you mention it, yes. But it's not for me,' she began.

'Who else would it be for?' Richard's eyes narrowed suspiciously – Cassie wondered if there might even be a hint of jealousy there too. 'You'd better start from the beginning.'

'Well,' Cassie sighed. 'I think it might be easier if I just showed you . . .'

'Cassie, what the hell . . . ?'

Richard had grown more and more impatient and curious as Cassie led him towards Ranjit's room, glancing furtively over her shoulder to make sure nobody saw them. She couldn't help being reminded of the night Sir Alric had made his own big reveal.

'Where are you taking me?' Richard said again. 'I mean, I can't pretend I'm not hoping you're finding a secluded spot to have your way with me.'

'Richard . . .'

'You're not an axe murderer, are you? I knew there was something about you – I thought it was a great personality and stunning good looks, but maybe, just maybe, it's that you're a psychopath and—'

'Richard! Shhh. We're here, OK?'

They were standing once more outside the ornately carved door. Richard let out a low whistle, clearly intrigued. Cassie cleared her throat nervously, but just as she reached out to turn the door handle, they heard a groan come from inside. Gasping, Cassie wrenched the door wide and rushed inside. The bread roll and cheese tumbled free of the napkin as she dropped it and flew to Ranjit's side.

'Ranjit!'

She was aware of Richard standing beside her, struck dumb, but all she could do was hold Ranjit's face, stroking it with her thumbs, kissing his forehead. 'Ranjit, wake up! Ranjit!'

'Jesus, Cassie,' breathed Richard. 'Where the hell did you find him?'

'Well, I'm not surprised you were in trouble with Sir Alric.'

Richard was pacing the room, shaking his head in disbelief. 'You are one crazy chick, Cassie Bell. You might as well have handed a loaded gun to Katerina. How did you get away?'

'They were so preoccupied with the artefacts, I managed to distract them for long enough for us to get out of there.' In a shamed murmur she added, 'I guess once Brigitte and Katerina had those, they didn't need us any more.'

'It's not your fault,' he consoled her. 'What were you supposed to do?'

'Needless to say that's not how Sir Alric sees it.' Cassie rubbed her face with both hands. 'Oh, Richard. What a bloody mess.'

'Not entirely. You've got Sleeping Beauty back, haven't you?'

True. She turned and gazed at Ranjit again, when he opened his eyes and emitted another low groan. She leaned over him, almost afraid to touch him, watching him closely. She reached down gripping his hand, and was relieved to feel his fingers tighten around hers. It seemed he was finally coming around properly.

'Cassie . . . ?'

'Oh my God,' she whispered. 'You're all right.' She flung her arms around Ranjit, and without thinking her lips found his. He returned her kiss urgently, and in the same instant she felt her spirit leap to life, flaming passionately, burning for him—

'Ahem.'

Coming to her senses, Cassie pulled away, flushing with embarrassment as she heard Richard pointedly clear his throat. Looking back towards Ranjit, she noticed he looked as shocked as she did, and she could see his pulse still thrashing in his throat. He put his hands to his head, shaking it slowly.

'I'm— What happened?'

His eyes were roaming the room, perplexed and still a little dazed, but showing a dawning horror. Ranjit must suspect, she thought, that she'd brought him to the very

188

place he didn't want to be. And as he suddenly caught sight of the boy behind Cassie, his gaze focused and his eyes widened with certainty.

'Richard?' he whispered. With Cassie's help he pulled himself half up. 'What are *you*—'

Richard had taken an involuntary step back, his expression nervous, but Ranjit only looked at him, bleary and confused. Then his shoulders sagged.

'I'm at the Academy, aren't I?' he asked, looking up at Cassie. She nodded silently.

Ranjit sighed, and turned back to Richard. 'And you're . . .' he began hoarsely, then swallowed. 'You're OK.'

'Not for want of you trying,' Richard replied wryly, remembering the events in Istanbul. Ranjit was still blinking, struggling to get the words out.

'I'm sorry. I didn't mean—'

'No, you didn't,' Cassie told him firmly. 'It wasn't your fault.'

Ranjit slumped back. There was despair in his expression. 'That isn't true.'

'It is.' She wanted to shake him. 'It was because of the Pendant. Don't you understand? It was cursed. Anyone who touched it first would have done what you did.'

A mirthless smile twitched the corner of Ranjit's

mouth. 'I'd like to think that's true.'

'You're telling me you meant to try and kill me?' Richard raised his hands in mock horror.

'Stop fooling, Halton-Jones.' Ranjit turned his head and stared bleakly at Richard. 'You know how close I came.'

Richard nodded, sobering. 'I know it. But it's like Cassie says: it wasn't really you.'

Ranjit glared at him, propping himself up once more on his elbows. Cassie put her arm round his shoulders to help him, but he shook her off with a shiver. Cassie's heart ached at the gesture.

'Excuses,' Ranjit growled. 'I couldn't have done any of that if there hadn't been something inside me that wanted to. Part of me must have wanted to kill you, Richard.'

Richard shrugged lightly. 'Part of you probably still does. Why should you be any different to half the school?'

Ranjit choked a weak laugh, but there was a taint of despair in it. For the first time he allowed himself to gaze directly into Cassie's eyes. 'Curse or no curse, I'm a murderer.'

'No, listen, Ranjit. You—'

'You can't put a gloss on it! I killed Yusuf and I killed Mikhail. And . . . and I killed— Oh, God, you must hate me.' He put his hands over his face.

'Ranjit, no—'

'I can still hardly believe I did what I did in Istanbul, Cassie, but it happened. God . . . Isabella? She must hate me more than anyone . . .'

Cassie shook her head, trying to make him stop. 'No! Ranjit! Listen, you don't understand—'

'I killed Jake. Cassie, I killed Jake.' Tears began to pool in his eyes and he quickly swiped them away, his head in his hands.

'*Ranjit!*' Cassie exclaimed, and he looked up. 'Listen to me! I know this is going to sound crazy . . . but Jake isn't dead!'

There was silence, then suddenly, a voice behind them.

'What?' exclaimed Richard.

Cassie had almost forgotten he was there. 'God, Richard. Yes, I'm sorry . . .'

She looked at him, staring open-mouthed and aghast, then returned her gaze pleadingly to Ranjit as he levered himself with huge effort to a sitting position. He swung his legs down and gripped the edge of the mattress to keep his swaying body straight. His eyes were feverishly brilliant, his skin even paler than before.

'Jake.' He began quietly, then cleared his throat and tried again. 'Jake. Isn't. Dead?'

'No. Jake's very much alive,' she said urgently.

Richard rubbed his neck, blowing out a disbelieving breath. 'Anything else you haven't mentioned, C? Have you got my pet Labrador from when I was eight years old hidden under the bed?'

'I'm really sorry. I couldn't tell anyone, Richard, I wasn't allowed.' She swallowed hard and clutched Ranjit's hand, squeezing it. 'Darke saved him. With the Tears.'

Ranjit didn't say anything for a long time, but she saw his jaw clenching, his brow furrowed. 'Good. That's really good,' he said at last. 'I'm so glad. It doesn't change much. I still killed the others . . .' His eyes filmed with tears again, but he gritted his teeth as he held them back.

'Jesus, Ranjit.' Cassie sat down beside him and took him in her arms. 'Look at you. Look how much remorse you have. These were your friends, your classmates – no matter how you felt about them before the Curse, you'd *never* have done something like that unless it was out of your control. Don't you see how that proves it? How often do we have to tell you? It wasn't you.'

Ranjit lifted his palms and glared at them as if they were soaked in blood. 'To hell with it,' he whispered. 'I can't undo it. I don't want to go in the damned Confine, so I guess I'll just have to keep running. I can't stay here. Where exactly is the Academy anyway?'

Cassie bit her lip. 'Kenya.'

'Jesus,' Ranjit sighed. 'I need to get out of here.'

'Honestly, Singh,' Richard pointed out scathingly, 'Cassie here has just saved your arse, so don't be an ingrate. Cool your jets for a moment, spend a little time.'

Ranjit got unsteadily to his feet, then, when he had his balance, raked his hands through his hair. He stared down at Cassie, who met his gaze, her heart pounding to feel him standing over her, tall and handsome despite his weakness. He seemed to have to actively tear himself away as he limped over to the French windows and pulled the thin curtain aside.

'Listen, Ranjit, don't worry,' she said, going to stand by his side. 'You're safe here. Sir Alric knows what happened, everything. He knew about the Curse to start with; if this is anyone's fault, it's his. And he'll sort things out, I swear he will. He'll fix everything with the Council. There won't be any question of the Confine or anything like that, I promise. Besides, nobody else knows you're here – no one even knows this room exists besides Darke, Isabella, Jake.'

But instead of seeming relieved, Ranjit blanched, a light of hideous understanding dawning in his eyes. He reached out and grabbed Cassie's arm. 'Oh God.' He rubbed his face with his free hand. 'Where is he? Where's Darke?'

'He isn't here,' Cassie told him. 'You've got time to

recover, time to think before we make our next move. He's gone to get his papers at the Mount Kenya lodge. We, uh, we need to figure out what to do next about . . .' She couldn't say their names.

'Cassie! I only just remembered. Brigitte. Katerina!'

'Yes, but we're going to figure out how to—'

'Cassie, no. Did you . . . did you say you . . .' He seized her again, shook her. 'Tell me you didn't give them the artefacts!'

Her silence must have told him everything.

He went entirely still, searching her face as if even now she could tell him she was kidding. 'Oh, God, Cassie. No. This is a catastrophe.'

'Hey,' interrupted Richard indignantly. 'She gave them up for you!'

'I know. I know.' Ranjit rubbed his temples hard. Impulsively, he reached out and put his hands on her shoulders, then pulled her into a hesitant embrace.

Cassie closed her eyes, leaning the side of her head against his shoulder, revelling in the closeness even as they both stiffened, trying to hold back. Eventually she pulled away.

'We're going to get them back,' she told him, more confidently than she felt.

'There may not be time for that,' said Ranjit dully. 'It

may already have happened.'

'What might have happened?' She frowned, staring at Ranjit quizzically, but feeling a growing sense of dread. 'What do you know?'

'They had the Urn once they'd kidnapped me, of course. But they needed the Knife and the Pendant to complete their plan. They explained it to me, the whole damn thing. Gloating, of course. They assumed I'd be dead by now.'

'And?' prompted Richard impatiently.

'They need to get a spirit out of the Urn.'

Cassie swallowed nervously. 'So it does still contain a spirit? One the Eldest trapped there?'

'Worse. Much worse.' Ranjit leaned both hands against the panes of the French windows and stared bleakly out towards the ocean. 'The spirit in the Urn? *It's the Eldest himself.*'

CHAPTER SEVENTEEN

Cassie pulled her hair off her face and took great gulps of oxygen into her lungs, trying to swerve her mind away from the consequences she might already have brought about.

'I don't get it. I thought the Eldest was driven away by the Council? And without the artefacts he couldn't feed on other Few. That's why they *hid* the Urn, isn't it, as well as all the other artefacts?'

'That's the story they put about,' said Ranjit darkly. 'Apparently what really happened was that they lured him to his own Urn and imprisoned him there. They didn't want the true story to get out, because inevitably the Eldest's followers would seek him out and try to free him. And now they have found him.'

They'd risked venturing on to the balcony because they all needed air, though Ranjit looked downright dizzy with it. He needed to feed – properly – Cassie thought vaguely, but they hadn't even got to that yet, with all the revelations that were happening. She, Ranjit and Richard stood watching the glitter and roll of the turquoise waves, listening to the birdsong and the screech of monkeys and the clatter from the dining room far below on the ground floor.

'But to free the Eldest? Surely even our Katerina isn't that stupid,' remarked Richard hopefully.

'They're bound to free him, or try to,' said Cassie dully. 'The Svenssons are nuts.'

'And . . . and if they do it'll be chaos. Carnage.' Ranjit put an arm round her shoulders as if that could soften his words. 'He'll start with the Few, but he won't stop there. The whole world will be his feeding trough. But he'll need a very strong host . . . I wonder what they're planning exactly regarding that? Maybe one of them, even?' He shook his head incredulously. 'Can you imagine the Eldest in a position of power? Congress, maybe, or even the Presidency?'

'I can't. I don't want to.' Cassie ground her teeth. 'We have to stop them.'

'Listen, you're not to blame, Cassie. You couldn't know.'

'Uh-huh. And remember how you reacted when I told

you the same thing? Well, multiply that by a hundred.'

'Aren't we rather wasting time with a mutual blame society?' drawled Richard. 'Try Sir Alric again.'

Cassie pulled out her phone and thumbed in his number yet again. She glanced from Ranjit to Richard as she held it to her ear. 'Still going to voicemail. Dammit.'

'Try the lodge,' suggested Richard.

'I didn't want to bring Isabella and Jake into this, but—' Reluctantly Cassie pressed the entry for Sir Alric's safari lodge, then raised her eyebrows. 'It's dead.'

'That doesn't sound good,' said Ranjit, frowning with concern.

Cassie hesitated, not wanting to think the worst. 'The phone system isn't that reliable . . .'

'I'll tell you what *is* reliable,' said Richard. 'My favourite toy. Come on. Let's stop wasting time. We're going to the airstrip.'

Cassie was out of her seat before the Cessna had even bumped to a halt on the long flat strip of savannah. Ranjit was right behind her as she wrestled the door open to the dry, dusty heat of the day and had begun lowering the steps before Richard had taken off his headset. She couldn't explain the terrible urgency that had filled her since they'd snapped out of their inertia and decided to sneak out of the Academy and fly straight to Mount Kenya, but she knew she wanted to see Jake and Isabella with her own eyes: alive, well, and loved-up.

She bolted across the tracks and towards the lodge, terrified of what she might find – or might not find – but when she came in sight of the long veranda, she almost shrieked with relief. Jake sat on a rattan couch, a book in his hand; Isabella lay the length of it, her head on his lap and her own book over her face.

'Cassie?' Jake dropped his book casually over the arm of the couch, and Isabella, startled awake, pulled the book off her face and sat up.

'Jake! Isabella!' Cassie slowed to a walk, trying and failing to look a little more casual. 'Is everything . . . OK?' she panted.

They didn't answer. Both of them were on their feet now, staring beyond Cassie.

'Oh—' Isabella gasped, then flung her hands over her mouth. Jake froze.

Cassie glanced over her shoulder, momentarily dumbfounded.

Of course. Behind her stood Ranjit, his gaze remorseful and stricken. At his side, Richard glanced with interest from him to Jake and back.

Cassie rubbed her hand across her head and breathed out. 'Oh. Isabella, can we come in? We've got a lot to tell you . . .'

Jake was pacing the rug in front of the fireplace, casting dumbfounded looks at Ranjit, who sat between Richard and Cassie on the leather sofa. Isabella was perched on the arm next to Cassie, her hand lightly on her best friend's shoulder.

'It's a lot to take in,' muttered Jake, 'that's all.'

'I know,' said Ranjit. 'I'm sorry.' He glanced at Isabella. 'You've no idea how sorry.'

'I heard you the first time.' Jake came to an abrupt halt. 'You said a lot of stuff that night, Ranjit. When you "killed" me. A lot of stuff about what happened with Jess in Cambodia.'

Ranjit put his head in his hands. 'I didn't mean any of it. I never meant for it to happen. I never meant Jessica any harm. Or you, for that matter.'

'And as for you . . .' Jake glowered at Richard. 'The part you played in Jessica's death? You *knew* what you were doing when you held up Ranjit. When you—'

'Jake?' Isabella interrupted, standing up and going across to him. She slid her arms around his waist. 'Can I say something?'

'Yeah.' Taken aback, he put an arm round her shoulders.

'It seems to me there's only one person who really knew what she was doing the night Jess died, and it wasn't Ranjit. It wasn't even Keiko.'

'I knew what I was doing,' put in Richard softly, and Cassie took his hand and squeezed it. 'I did delay Ranjit, long enough for Katerina to get to Jess . . .'

'Yes,' said Isabella, 'but you didn't know what would come of it. Jake, Richard had *no idea* what Katerina was planning. It's Katerina who's truly responsible for Jessica's death, and if what Cassie says is right, she could be responsible for a lot more. We're all of us in schlock—'

'Shock,' muttered Cassie absently.

'Shock, then. But we don't have any more time to waste. We have to get hold of Sir Alric, and fast.'

'His mobile's off,' said Cassie bleakly. 'We'll just have to wait for him. Where the hell is he?' She checked her watch again.

Isabella stared at her. 'His phone is never switched off when he's here at the lodge. He told us that, in case we needed to contact him.'

Cassie's heart dipped. 'Do you have any idea where he went?'

Isabella exchanged a worried look with Jake. 'He didn't

say. He left three quarters of an hour ago.'

'With Marat,' said Jake.

Cassie felt the blood drain from her face. 'Marat was here?' She thought back to the squat man's face in the office after she'd stolen the artefacts. This couldn't be good. 'I don't trust him.'

'Who does?' muttered Jake. 'Except for Sir Alric.'

Ranjit stood up. 'What was he doing before he left? Why did he go out?'

'Hard to say. He's been buried in his study since he arrived yesterday. I asked what he was looking for, and when he'd finished barking at me, he said even he didn't exactly know. Just that he'd know when he found it.'

Cassie tried to contain her frustration. 'Well, he must have found something if he went out.'

Jake rubbed his temples, giving Isabella a worried glance. 'Maybe. Marat turned up about an hour ago, and they disappeared into the study, then Sir Alric stuck his head round the door and said they were going out together to investigate a lead.'

'A lead?' murmured Cassie. So Marat had suddenly turned up bearing news? And now Sir Alric had gone off with him somewhere he couldn't get a mobile signal? Don't panic, she told herself as the feeling rose up. She had to keep a clear head.

Without another word, Cassie headed for the door at the side of the vast lounge. 'This is his study, right?'

'Yeah.' Jake was at her side, pushing open the door.

'Oh my God,' whispered Cassie.

All four of them stood staring at the chaos on the desk and the floor. Papers had been tossed aside, left higgledy-piggledy on tables. Heaps of them had slid off the desk into piles on the rug. Filing cabinet drawers stood open, the files still open on top.

'Jesus,' murmured Richard. 'What's this impostor done with our favourite control freak?'

Cassie shook her head. 'It must have been something urgent. What was he looking for?'

'What did he *find*?' murmured Ranjit darkly.

'We've got to go after him,' said Cassie, turning to go.

'Hang on, Cassie. Can't do that till we find where he went.' Ranjit touched her arm. Even in the circumstances Cassie felt her skin prickle and her blood leap in response. Glancing at him, she met golden eyes that were as shocked by his own reaction as she was by hers. Gently she shook him off. There was no time for this.

'There's got to be something here.' Richard yanked out a desk drawer.

Isabella heaved a deep sigh. 'Let's start looking.'

Cassie bent to lift a discarded pile of documents,

flicking through them as she dumped them on the desk. All the others had taken sheaves of paper, barely taking time to read each heading before moving on to the next. Isabella sat cross-legged on the floor, surrounded by files, her expression hopeless.

'Wait. Look,' said Jake, lifting a lined notebook and flipping it open. 'A bunch of notes about the Tears.' He peered at it, and Cassie saw a shadow flit across his face.

'What? What's it say?'

'Nothing. Doesn't help.' Still, Cassie noticed, he stuck it in the back pocket of his jeans. Well, he must be curious about the liquid that had saved his life.

'If it doesn't help, don't waste time on it,' she said sharply. 'Keep looking, everybody.'

Calm down, Cassie told herself. Calm down. We just have to look till we find.

The state of the room disturbed her, if only because of the likelihood that Sir Alric was responsible for the mess. This desperation wasn't like him – he was trying to find something, and quickly. What had Marat told him? Thinking about it now, Cassie was sure there was no one else who would have tried to burgle Sir Alric's office at the start of term. No student she knew of – not even the most arrogant of the Few – would have dared. That must have been Marat's first abortive attempt to steal the artefacts. She remembered his quiet satisfaction, his perfectly calm demeanour as he reordered Sir Alric's office after Cassie's burglary. Why had he done that? Why cover for her when he so disliked her?

Because, perhaps, she'd done his job for him?

But Marat, for all his sinister nature, never struck Cassie as the sort to act alone. He'd want a leader. And who else could that be but the Svenssons, given what had happened . . . ?

Her foot knocked against something solid, half-covered by the papers on the floor. The phone handset from Sir Alric's desk. Picking it up, thumbing buttons, she pressed it to her ear.

'Guys – the phone's completely dead. Not just off the hook, dead.'

A shiver ran down her spine at the thought of Sir Alric, alone in Marat's company out in the bush. Suddenly she stood up.

'That little git Marat's done something. He's in cahoots with Brigitte and Katerina, I'm sure of it. He's tricked Sir Alric, somehow, he must have. Nothing else would drag Sir Alric away if he was still searching his files, still unsure of exactly what he was looking for.'

Just as she said it, Jake was sweeping his arm across the papers on the desk, sending them tumbling to the floor in a disordered mess.

'Like that's going to help,' drawled Richard.

Jake just leaned on the desktop, staring at it. 'But it is,' he said, pointing down. 'There's a map.'

They clustered round the desk. Sure enough, beneath the papers, pinned flat under a protective glass top, was a large-scale map of the slopes of Mount Kenya. As they examined it, something caught Cassie's eye in the scattered papers Jake had just tossed aside, and she picked it carefully off the floor, narrowing her eyes.

'This looks pretty old,' she muttered, rubbing the document lightly with a thumb.

Ranjit peered over her shoulder. 'Something about a temple.' He took the fragile yellowed sheet from Cassie, laid it against the map beneath the glass. 'Same symbol. Look.'

'Not one I ever saw on the Ordnance Survey,' observed Richard. Sure enough, it was familiar to Cassie only in one respect: it resembled the broken symbol branded into her shoulder blade. As if to confirm her thoughts, Richard loosened his collar further and tugged his shirt down, turning so that they could all see the brand on his shoulder.

'Yes,' breathed Ranjit. 'It's the Few symbol.'

They all looked at each other. Jake worked his fingers

underneath the desktop glass and yanked it up, pushing it away until it slid on to the floor with a crack like a gunshot. It hadn't shattered, but a clean crack ran from corner to corner.

Jake loosened the map from the desk, picking at the edges that had stuck to the wood. When it was free, he folded it carefully to show the patch of contours with the unfamiliar symbol at its centre.

'Mount Kenya,' he said. 'You think that's it? Where he's gone?'

'We're never going to get a better clue.' Richard said.

'We've got to go for it,' said Ranjit. 'Come on.'

Ranjit, Richard and Isabella were already out of the door, but uncharacteristically Jake hung back, and Cassie paused to urge him to hurry.

But just as she opened her mouth, she saw him snatch a small container from a side table and stuff it into his pocket. His eyes met hers, and she shut her mouth. She wasn't going to ask. They didn't have time.

'Right,' he said grimly. 'Now let's go.'

CHAPTER EIGHTEEN

As they climbed the steep-sided valley through the forest, Cassie could hear Isabella rasping for breath, but clearly her friend had no intention of being left behind. Despite the lazy weeks with Jake, and the aimless period of grief before then, she was grimly keeping up with three Few and her hyper-conditioned boyfriend.

Dusk was falling swiftly, but Cassie led the way, occasionally pausing impatiently so that Ranjit could check the map. As they waited on a basalt outcrop for Isabella to catch up, she caught sight of Ranjit's eyes glowing behind her in the gathering darkness. From the odd look she got from Isabella as she pulled her up the steep rock, she guessed her own eyes looked much the same. Their Few power was primed – they weren't sure exactly what they were about to face.

'Are we sure this is a good idea? If we go much higher

the altitude's going to be a problem for Isabella,' Richard muttered to the others in a low voice.

'Me too,' admitted Jake, 'but it's not much further. According to the map, anyway. If we're even going to the right place.'

'Let's just hope we're not too late,' Cassie replied, clenching her jaw. This was all her fault – who knows what Marat and the Svenssons had planned for Sir Alric. They had to get to them as quickly as possible. 'Come on, we've got to keep moving,' she urged.

Cassie led them on quickly, listening out for the sounds of the forest: scurrying rodents in the undergrowth, the distant roar of a river, the high-pitched night chorus of cicadas. Between the trunks of the dense trees, the sky was turning from crystal blue to a deep amber, and in the occasional glimpses Cassie got of the ragged peak of Mount Kenya, the snow and glaciers were streaked with blue shadow and tinged with gold. It wouldn't be long before the light died from the peak altogether, and true darkness fell in the forest.

As they hurried onwards, Ranjit hesitated again, checking the map, and Cassie pulled up and turned to watch him. Richard paused too, and Jake and Isabella caught up, Jake reaching out and taking his girlfriend's hand to make sure she was close.

'Here,' Ranjit said in a low voice. 'Cassie, three steps back. Look.'

The slit in the volcanic rock was almost imperceptible through the dense trees, and she doubted it would have been any more obvious in full daylight; as it was, it could easily have been taken for a stripe of deeper shadow, or a vein of blacker rock. Shoving branches aside, Ranjit crouched and forced his way across a ridge of stone, and Cassie followed, with the others at her heels.

'We're not the first to come here tonight,' Ranjit said grimly.

Sure enough, there were signs of disturbance. Cassie touched broken twigs, then ran the palm of her hand down the rock. A breath of air, cold and dank, whispered from the hole across her skin, and she snatched her hand away. Ranjit caught it, linking his fingers with hers. His gaze met hers, intense and searching.

'Are you ready, Cassie?'

'As I'll ever be.' She smiled at him, and suddenly the fear was gone. Her blood stirred hot inside her, and it wasn't only the proximity of Ranjit. There were enemies to crush, she thought; a theft to repay, revenge to be taken. Her fingertips tingled in his hand, and he squeezed them slightly, his mouth crooking at one corner.

Yes, he felt it too.

Like old times! came the voice from inside her. We're in it together!

Leaning forward recklessly, Cassie kissed Ranjit's lips. He tightened his grip on her hand, drew her closer, returned her kiss. Blood stirred in her veins, her nerves crackled, and her heart leaped, suddenly too big for her all-too-human ribcage.

Reluctantly pulling away, she turned back to the gap in the rock-face. They were still holding hands as she shouldered her way through the slender opening and was swallowed by blackness.

'I don't want to use the torch if we can help it,' came Jake's murmur in the black coldness.

'I don't think we'll have to,' was Ranjit's whispered reply. 'Wait a bit. There's some light up ahead.'

Cassie realised he was right; her Few-sharpened eyes were already registering shapes and edges and the faintest phosphorescent glow. She, Richard and Ranjit were the first to notice it; Jake and Isabella took a little longer to adjust, but at last they were advancing into the tunnels with reasonable confidence, given the uncertainty of what they were heading towards . . .

Sensing something moving above her, Cassie halted. The roof of the tunnel was not high, but even in the

211

faintest of light she could make out things that were stirring, writhing. At her side Richard followed her stare.

'It's like . . .' he whispered.

'. . . the Arc de Triomphe temple,' Cassie finished for him, remembering with a shiver her initiation in the bowels of that underground cavern below the busiest roundabout in Paris. If such a secret could exist there, what might they find below the primordial geology of Mount Kenya? Deliberately Cassie averted her gaze from the eerily moving rock above her, and focused ahead.

She couldn't even guess at how far they'd come beneath the rock; distance and time were impossible to estimate in this enclosed lightless place. She could feel her heart thumping in her chest with tense anticipation. When would this tunnel end? But at last Ranjit put a hand on her shoulder to bring her to a sudden halt.

'Up ahead,' he murmured, barely audibly. 'I feel them.'

Cassie waited for a tremor of fear, but it didn't materialise. Instead she felt her lip curl with contempt, all her muscles tensing in anticipation. She clenched and flexed her fists.

Ranjit was right. The light was growing far stronger here; and at its heart was a sinister greenish glow. Backing up against the walls, Cassie waited as the others caught up. She jerked her thumb to indicate the unseen space beyond the next corner, and then quickly pressed a finger to her lips. Surprise was one of their only advantages.

The faint ethereal light pulsated as she crept up silently and peered around the corner. Her breath caught in her throat, and behind her Ranjit gave her shoulder a quick, questioning squeeze. She turned back to him, her eyes wide with anger.

'Look,' she whispered through gritted teeth.

He peered past her, and took a horrified breath.

In a cave-like opening, they could see four figures – Sir Alric was down on the ground struggling, lashing out, but Brigitte and Katerina were savagely tightening chains around his wrists; Cassie thought the gleaming metal looked familiar, and realised they were like the chains that had held her during her own initiation. In a dark corner, Cassie could make out the stocky figure of Marat, standing off to the side, observing his employer dispassionately. Sir Alric's movements were slow and ineffectual; he looked groggy, bruised and bloodied, and the Svensson women were clearly in command as they hoisted him to his feet and began fastening him to some bolts in the cave wall using the chains.

Impulsively, Cassie began to lunge forward, only to feel Ranjit's hand grip her arm tightly. He pulled her back.

'Cassie, wait!' he hissed, pointing towards the dark glow beyond them.

She stared. The Urn was set in an elaborately carved alcove behind and above Sir Alric's head, and on either side of it lay the Pendant and the Knife. The Urn's translucent jade throbbed with that intense, brilliant glow Cassie had seen before, but around it hovered something else, a hideous light that seemed to emanate from it. It roiled and swirled, making twisted monstrous shapes of elusive smoke that regularly dissipated then coalesced into a single serpentine coil.

With a last yank on the chains binding Sir Alric, Brigitte turned and gazed up at the light with a kind of adoration.

'So close, Katerina. So close! He will be free!'

Something told Cassie they weren't talking about Sir Alric.

'Yes,' Katerina intoned. She turned and glared contemptuously at Sir Alric. 'Soon your spirit will be the Eldest's first good meal in centuries. And soon your body will be his *host*,' she spat. 'You should feel honoured.'

'Prepare the artefacts,' Brigitte told her daughter. Grimly, Cassie followed their gaze towards their altar of artefacts, and her eyes were drawn to the Knife beside it. Its carved creatures were alive, twisting, and it seemed to radiate a light all of its own, drawing her, calling to her, wanting her . . .

Unable to bear it a moment longer, Cassie tore her arm free of Ranjit's grasp and dived around the corner, heading straight towards the glowing alcove and the Knife. Brigitte spun on her heel, gaping.

'NO! Cassie!'

Ranjit's cry of warning was drowned out by a shriek of rage. Katerina hurtled towards Cassie, slamming into her and flinging her backwards. Cassie crashed hard into the solid rock wall, pain shooting through her shoulders and head, but she staggered back to her feet, snarling, and focused. Drawing up all her strength, she began to project her unusual power out beyond herself. The cave turned ruby-red in her vision, and she drew a triumphant breath to hurl the full force of it towards Katerina—

'Cassie! DON'T DO THAT!'

But Sir Alric's yell of horror was cut off abruptly; Marat stepped from the shadows and snapped his head back with a vicious punch. Still, his brief shout was enough to make Cassie pause, and she rocked back on her heels, surprised and confused.

Beyond Katerina, the Urn was brightening, its light focusing into a single dazzling beam that lanced out towards Cassie like a laser. Shocked, Cassie tried to refocus her power against it, but instead of combating the strange light, she found herself frozen, rooted to the spot. The Urn's green light enveloped her.

'Don't . . . !' mumbled Sir Alric again. But it was too late.

Katerina stalked over to stand before Cassie, but she didn't launch a new attack. She didn't have to. The girl was grinning with horrible delight, fists clenched as she gazed at the immobilised Cassie.

'Oh, yes, Cassie Bell!' she howled. 'Yes! By all means do!'

CHAPTER NINETEEN

Cassie wanted to scream with futile rage, but she couldn't even do that. Horror swamped her as she stared down at her own chest.

She'd projected her spirit beyond her body – her special power, her unique power – and now it was going to be the death of her. The Urn's light was almost unbearably bright now; with a sinking realisation, Cassie deduced that the Eldest was consuming her projected spirit, absorbing its energy. She was growing weaker by the minute.

'Cassie!' She heard Ranjit's howl as if from a great distance.

No . . . came the echo from inside her own head. No . . . !

But she was powerless as her friends rushed forward. Yelling with fury, Ranjit, Richard, Jake and Isabella were suddenly all around her. They were trying to protect her, she knew – to stop this from happening. But it seemed hopeless, and she could do nothing to help, nothing to save herself. Slowly, inexorably, her power was draining away into the Urn. She let out a growl of pure frustration but could still say nothing, could not move.

She watched helplessly as Marat whacked his fist into the side of Isabella's head and she went stumbling down. Jake flew at Marat, trying to protect her, but the stocky little man turned with shocking fluidity, ducked and then slammed his fist into Jake's jaw. The American boy went down like a stone, and Marat smirked. A few metres away Richard was doing his damnedest to lash out at Katerina, but she and her mother, fierce with joy, overwhelmed him with blows.

Ranjit gripped Cassie's arms, trying to wrench her free from the Eldest's hold; his hands hissed with green smoke where they touched her skin, and at last he gave a cry of pain and fell back. Cassie's eyes met his, and he shook his head in despair. Beside him Richard had been struck to the ground, and Ranjit rolled over and sprang up to defend him just as Brigitte moved in for a killing blow.

I . . . don't want . . . to die, Cassandra!

Me either, Estelle.

And she didn't want her friends to die, either. All the

power inside her, and she couldn't save her friends. All that power . . .

Not all, my dear!

Estelle . . .

Oh, my darling Cassandra! You haven't got a choice any more. We haven't got a choice! It's the end if you don't. For all of us.

Cassie shut her eyes tight, then, gritting her teeth, she blinked back the despair that had threatened to overwhelm her. She knew what she had to do – had to try, it was the only way . . .

Come on then, Estelle. COME IN!

For . . . once and for . . . all, my dear?

YES!

Cassie's head was flung back with the impact of the spirit entering her. Eyes wide, she stared at the writhing cavern ceiling, feeling the blissful power of the whole spirit slamming into her veins, racing like a fizzing tide.

Yes!

Cassie gave a howl of ecstasy, realising that she was free, able to move again, able to shout. Energy poured back into her limbs, and the pain was gone as if Estelle had turned a switch. Cassie's mind felt bright and clear and piercing, and power pulsed in her chest. Around and inside her there was a horrible screeching, but she knew it wasn't coming from her. It was coming from the eldritch green glow, the light of the Eldest.

'GET AWAY FROM US!' she screamed.

Then, abruptly, the beam of light snapped, twitching and vanishing from around her. Cassie felt a single piercing explosion of relief and triumph.

And then she crumpled to the floor.

Ranjit saw her fall. With one last savage slash at Katerina, he turned and rushed to Cassie's side. Despite her feeling of utter strength just moments ago, it was clearly short-lived. Estelle's spirit-power was hugely drained, and now Cassie's breath was coming in ragged gasps, her muscles now as weak as a month-old kitten's, but she managed to croak, 'No, Ranjit. Stop her—'

Too late. Katerina had darted to Sir Alric and now she gripped his hair and yanked his head back. His eyes were filmy and blurred, and blood trickled thickly from his nostrils.

There was too much blood on Ranjit's face, too, and though his teeth were bared in fury, the scarlet taint of his eyes was fading with exhaustion. He managed to get his arms around Cassie and help her stumble on to all fours.

'No,' she gasped.

The swirling light around the Urn was intensifying again. There was a roaring in her ears now, from the strange pulsating light above them all and from her own brain. Under its intense dazzle, Brigitte kicked the defeated Richard aside and paced to Sir Alric's chained form. She slammed her fist into his face, and blood spattered her.

'And now,' she said with a hiss of contempt, turning to Katerina but still gripping Sir Alric's hair. 'Now, my daughter. We'll finish this.'

'Don't do it!' yelled Ranjit. 'You don't know what you're doing!'

'Of course we do! You stupid, weak fools!' Brigitte's voice seared Cassie's brain. 'There's nothing you can do! The Eldest will feed on you *all*! Give in to him now and maybe it won't be such utter torture!'

Her daughter screamed with laughter. 'Mother! He'll like it more if it hurts them!'

Brigitte joined in the howls of hilarity, and even Marat behind them was cracking a smile. Viciously, the older woman grinned at Cassie and Ranjit, and grabbed Sir Alric's hair as Katerina let it go.

'You haven't got away with it, Bell. Fear not, once Darke's spirit is consumed and the Eldest has his body as a host, you will be next. I'm so glad we didn't kill you at Gedi!'

'Leave him alone!' yelled Cassie.

'Oh? Leave him alone?' Katerina shrieked, almost

hysterical now. 'He's the most powerful Few we could get our hands on, you stupid bitch! When he's fed on Darke's spirit, the Eldest will be unbeatable! Of course we're not going to leave him alone!' The blonde girl doubled over with crazed laughter, then reached up and whipped the Pendant from its place beside the Urn.

It swung from Katerina's hand, glinting with a brilliance that jade shouldn't possess. As it steadied and stilled, Katerina brandished the Pendant above Sir Alric's wrenched-back head. His mouth opened in a scream that never sounded. Cassie watched in horror as a faint white light began to spiral out from between his lips – they were drawing his spirit out using the ancient artefact. It drifted, grew denser, curled up into the dank air towards the intensifying light of the Eldest hovering above the Urn. Sir Alric began to struggle, but Brigitte held firm.

'Do not resist,' hissed Brigitte, shaking Darke's head as she tightened her grip on his hair. 'I'll be happy to submit to your authority once you host the Eldest, though.' She giggled, almost girlishly. 'I've always rather liked your body . . .'

She tailed off, and with a flourish she reached over and drew the Knife. The coil of white light was extended now to a thin and despairing tendril curling around the Pendant, and it was beginning to pull Sir Alric's body with it. His throat stretched, his back arched, and Brigitte grinned, raising the blade high to sever his spirit from his body.

'Ranjit, we have to DO SOMETHING!' Cassie cried, half-stumbling as she tried to get to Sir Alric herself.

Ranjit sprang to his feet again, his face etched with fury and a killing determination. He flew past Cassie, launching himself at Katerina, slamming her aside so that she crashed into her mother. Flung off balance, Brigitte dropped the Knife. It skidded towards Isabella, who held the unconscious Jake in her arms. But Isabella didn't need her hands. With savage accuracy, she kicked the Knife across the smooth stone floor back to Ranjit.

Ranjit snatched it up and in one fluid movement struck out at the chains on Sir Alric's wrists, shattering the links with a single blow. The man collapsed to the ground, and Ranjit caught him, but to do so he had to let go of the Knife, and Cassie watched in anguish as it spun across the floor again.

Brigitte, shrieking, flung herself on to the floor and snatched up the ethereal blade. Cassie had no hope of stopping her; she could only crawl to meet Ranjit, seizing Sir Alric's body from him, helping to drag him further away.

Brigitte rose to her feet, and with a hideous grin ran at

them once more. Cassie tried desperately to move her body to protect Sir Alric, but Ranjit was just in time to spin, lashing out with a blow that caught Brigitte's snarling face with an audible crack. Still clutching the Knife, the blonde woman was flung backwards through the air and slammed hard against the alcove that held the Urn. It wobbled under her impact, swung wildly, and then crashed to the ground.

The light within the jade Urn flickered; in harmony with it, the light of the Eldest vibrated and throbbed above them. Squealing, Brigitte reached protectively for the fallen Urn, but as she scrabbled on to all fours, she dropped it again.

But then she was no longer looking at the Urn. She was staring down at her own chest. For a moment everything seemed to go quiet.

'Mother?' howled Katerina, her voice echoing in the fallen silence.

Brigitte turned slowly, staggering, her face distorted with terror.

Rubbing sweat and blood from her eyes, Cassie saw something sticking out from the woman's breast. A broad twist of carved figures that now leaped to life, writhing and squirming against her body.

The hilt of the Knife.

Life was draining from Brigitte's pale face even as they watched. Her skin dried and shrank, tightening over her bones like a mummy's. It darkened and shrivelled until her eyes and screaming mouth were only hollows in a skull-mask. Cassie stared in horror as the white light of Brigitte's spirit curled out of her mouth and up, up towards the ceiling.

It hesitated, twisting and writhing as if in pain, or denial, but it was drifting now, sucked faster and faster towards the hovering spirit of the Eldest.

'M-Mother? Wait!' shrieked Katerina. 'Eldest, please!'

Marat had stepped forward and was gazing up at the colliding spirits with awe and not a little admiration. And then the small white breath of Brigitte's was abruptly engulfed in the Eldest. The glowing green light exploded with energy, and throbbed once more into new life.

As Brigitte's body crumbled to dust, shattering on to the ground, the Knife clattered to the rocky floor.

The greenish light coalesced again. It floated, every second seeming to grow denser. And then, with a howl like the sound of a thousand demons, it whipped free of the fallen Urn altogether, and the light in its jade walls went out.

The Eldest was a compact comet of light, now,

thrashing wildly above them, darting, seeking, desperate for a host.

'Katerina!' shouted Cassie. 'Drop the Pendant!'

Katerina's hands were over her mouth as she stared disbelievingly at the dust that was once her mother, and she made a horrible, high-pitched sound. Then, abruptly, she fell silent, and looked up at the Eldest above her, balling into a tight small sun of energy.

There was icy determination in her face as she ignored Cassie and raised the Pendant above her head. 'Eldest! Take me! Take me!'

Ranjit lunged, but before he could reach the Swedish girl, her mouth opened wide. The white light of her spirit shot out towards the Pendant, rapid and willing, making its jade glow brilliantly.

The dazzling ball of energy that was the Eldest had come to a dead stop above her, and now it expanded, sucking her spirit greedily into its growing luminous heart. The dreadful howling sound intensified too, and there was a brutal gargling sensation as Katerina's spirit was wrenched from her body, with no Knife poised to sever it cleanly. Then, in an instant, the coil of Katerina's spirit snapped and vanished.

She stood rigid, staring, her mouth still open in that silent scream. Above her the Eldest twisted and dived.

And then, still howling that dreadful demonic note, it vanished down into Katerina's gaping mouth.

The Svensson girl went entirely still, arms hanging loose. They all did, in the sudden, appalling silence. The Pendant fell from her lifeless fingers, clattering to the stone floor, its light extinguished like the Urn's.

Eventually, Cassie heard a strangled gasp behind her. Isabella, still with Jake in her protective arms, was staring in disbelief at the lifeless form of Katerina.

'Is . . . is she . . . dead?'

Cassie couldn't answer; her mouth was too dry, her breath stuck in her windpipe. Ranjit took a step towards Katerina's immobile body, but then halted.

She had begun to move again.

The silver-blonde hair seemed to shine brighter than ever as Katerina's neck turned, nightmarishly, almost experimentally. Again the head turned, to face the other way and smile at Marat. The porter seemed frozen, ecstatic, his breath caught in wonder. Facing forward once more, Katerina lifted her chin, then touched her cheeks gently with her hands.

A manicured nail found the vicious scar that Cassie had put on her cheekbone. Katerina frowned, drew a line along it with her fingertip, and the scar faded, and vanished.

She tilted her now-perfect face, and bestowed her evil smile on Isabella.

'Dead?' she murmured. 'Why, Miss Caruso. I'm only just getting started.'

CHAPTER TWENTY

'K-Katerina?' whispered Cassie as the girl got smoothly to her feet.

'Yes. And no. But mostly no.' The voice coming from Katerina's mouth was otherworldly, reverberating around the walls like rumbling thunder. Closing her eyes, Katerina raised her hands and gave a smile that was bursting with unbearable bliss. 'Katerina Svensson was a faithful disciple. She has given her body to host me, for which I am grateful. Though my host matters not. Subjugation will begin soon, and none shall surpass me.'

'She's . . .' Ranjit put his hands to his head. 'She's . . . The Eldest is in Katerina . . . ?'

Her face flicked round to him, grinning. 'I still feel her. But she is now . . . me.'

Richard was breathing hard as he took a step forward. And another. 'My God. Katerina.'

'No. Don't make me repeat myself.' The voice was a dangerous, rumbling hiss. 'Katerina Svensson is gone.'

Perfect lips drew back from white teeth, back further than was natural. The teeth grew jagged, and sleek sinewy muscles coiled and flexed under reptilian skin. Those crystal-blue eyes glowed with unearthly light, but it wasn't the usual scarlet Few light that Cassie knew so well: this piercing radiance was emerald-green, brimming with hate and ancient hunger.

Cassie had seen Katerina before in her monstrous form, but this wasn't it. It was far more terrifying. Cassie hadn't thought that was possible.

'And yet her form is perfect,' murmured the Eldest, stroking Katerina's slender arms. 'Perfect. In this host I shall be beautiful, deadly, unstoppable. Naturally I won't stop with her, but she is the best of beginnings.'

Cassie staggered to her feet, feeling strength begin to trickle back to her body at last as the spirit inside her rallied. And too late. She breathed hard through her clenched teeth. 'Wh-what do you mean, you won't stop?'

'I am *hungry*, Cassandra Bell. So very hungry, after so many centuries. I must feed, and feed again, on the strongest spirits and the strongest mortals.' She gave an elegant shrug, flexing her fingers. 'Then the weak ones will be all the easier to dominate. I shall . . . farm them as I take their world.'

'They'll stop you. We'll all stop you,' Isabella shouted, tightening her arms around the prostrate Jake. 'The world isn't like you remember it, you ugly creature. Even us mortals have weapons now.'

'I'm sure you do. I shall look forward to such a game. Perhaps you'll destroy each other, and save me the trouble. Now.' Curled talons beckoned to each of them in turn. 'Which of you will be the first to submit?' snarled the Eldest.

'In your dreams, Dark One.' Ranjit's sharp teeth were bared now too, and his eyes blazed. With no more warning, he flung himself at the monster.

The Eldest responded almost casually. Ranjit rebounded from her fist, giving a cry of pain and rage as his body skidded back. The Eldest stalked past him towards Isabella and Jake.

'NO!'

Cassie sprang at the Eldest now, feeling her own teeth bare like a wolf's. The Eldest turned to her, looking irritated, and even as Cassie lashed out with her fists and teeth and feet, she knew she was making no impression on the hideous creature. Languid claws raked her side and she screamed and fell back. Ranjit

231

caught her, and they rose together to face the oncoming monster.

But before they could do anything else, a burst of light and a colossal surge of power flung them back again, stunning them to the ground. Catching Ranjit's eye, she saw the twisted Few features fade, and he was a young man again, scared, but determined. And angry. Just like her. But what could they do?

I think we're going to die together, Ranjit . . .

Cassie felt herself lifted by unseen hands, then thrown hard to the ground so that the air was bashed out of her lungs. Dimly, she knew the same was happening to Ranjit; she could hear his ragged attempts to suck in one more lungful of oxygen, and then she was gasping too. Crawling towards him, she reached for his hand, but yet again they were torn apart and sent slamming into opposite walls. Cassie fell at Marat's feet; she caught his grin of satisfaction.

The Eldest was a looming shape above her. 'Katerina didn't like you, did she?' The voice was mocking. 'I can sense it.'

'Both of you can go to hell,' she mumbled through the blood in her mouth. 'If Katerina isn't there already.'

'Pah! You cannot defeat me. But there's power in you. Both of you. Strong spirits! I'll take that strength. Starting with you, little Cassandra. Who will stand against me then? Who?'

There was no breath in Cassie's lungs she could use to answer. As Marat kicked her forward, the Eldest stalked over to her beaten body. 'I asked you a question, worm! WHO?'

She braced herself for the pain; for the wrenching agony of her spirit and her life being ripped from her. But then a shadow stepped between her and the Eldest.

'I will. ME, you over-Botoxed prehistoric harpy.'

Richard Halton-Jones was standing in between them.

'Richard!' Cassie cried hoarsely. 'No!' She struggled to try and stand, desperate to stop him.

'She's quite right.' The Eldest mimicked her with that terrifying echo of a voice. ' "No, Richard!" '

But Richard stood firm, and Cassie gasped. There was something clutched in his hands and he raised it towards the Eldest. The Pendant.

The Eldest's eyes widened as they locked on the ancient artefact, and as she opened her mouth to speak again, her jaw seemed to lock. The features of her face twisted into a scowl, but instead of words, a low, ominous growl emitted from the Eldest's throat.

A bead of sweat trickled from Richard's temple, and he glanced sideways at Cassie, the corner of his lip quirking even now with desperate laughter. 'How does this bloody thing work, again?'

Cassie stumbled to a crouching position, hauling air into her lungs. 'Richard! Wh-what are you doing?'

The Pendant was pulsing with that intense light once more, and as Richard held it out towards the Eldest, Cassie realised that around Katerina's body, from head to toe, greenish-white light was beginning to ooze. The Eldest was squirming and writhing now, caught off guard by the Pendant's power.

'It's working!' Cassie shouted hopefully. 'You're drawing the spirit out of her!'

Slowly, painfully, the light was being sucked out from the Eldest's chest and mouth, and towards the carved jade. Screaming with rage, writhing against the Pendant's otherworldly pull, the Eldest focused on Richard, emerald eyes narrowing, teeth snapping. Still Richard held his ground, his arm shaking, the Pendant raised, his jaw clenched. Every muscle in his body seemed to be taut and shuddering, and he had to struggle to stay upright against both forces – the one flowing into the Pendant, and the raging intense fury of the Eldest.

'Cease . . . NOW!' she roared.

Richard wavered just for a moment, and the Eldest took her chance. She lunged towards him, claws raised, and struck him down with an almighty blow that rang and echoed from the cavern walls.

Cassie screamed.

Richard crumpled and the Pendant, its light extinguished, flew bumping and rolling away across the hard ground. Cassie ran towards Richard, but Ranjit raced for the Pendant, snatching it up.

'Cassie, get the Knife!'

For a fraction of a second she was torn, staring at Richard. But there was no help for him without stopping this nightmare. Gritting her teeth, Cassie dived for it.

She made it ahead of the Eldest with only a moment to spare, and snatched it up. The Knife's living hilt leaped back to life, fitting into her palm like an extension of her body. She roared and struck out at the Eldest wildly.

Opposite her, Ranjit raised the Pendant. The Eldest looked from him to Cassie, then back again, the first sign of panic in her glowing eyes. With the Knife on one side and the Pendant on the other, the Eldest was momentarily outmanoeuvred. She glared down at the tendril of spirit beginning to spiral from her ribcage towards the Pendant.

'No,' snarled the Eldest. 'No!'

Reaching down, she clutched at her own spirit with both hands. At her touch, it glowed poison-green, with a heart of brightest ruby.

'Very well,' she spat at Cassie and Ranjit. 'I'll deal with you both later.'

Suddenly, she clapped her hands together in the swirling spirit-light, and the cavern seemed to implode.

CHAPTER TWENTY-ONE

The world turned dark around Cassie, and a soundless impact slammed into her head, deafening her absolutely. For long seconds she thought the cave had collapsed, that she was being crushed beneath countless tons of volcanic rock.

Then, after agonising moments, seeping into her brain came the first sparks of consciousness. There was blinding light in the slits of her eyes, but as she forced them open she realised it was nothing but the phosphorescence of the cave. Pain seared through her head, and though she thought she was screaming, she could hear nothing. Cassie raised herself on to all fours, shaking her head furiously, blinking into the nothingness.

The Eldest had gone.

Isabella, staggering with dizziness, was hauling the groggy Jake to his feet, her mouth opening and closing as if she was coaxing him to rise; but Cassie could hear no sound coming from her either. Desperately she looked round for Ranjit. He was stumbling towards her, the Pendant still gripped in his fingers, also silently screaming her name. Cassie's brow furrowed.

Then she saw what lay a few metres to her left. Richard was a crumpled heap, like a broken puppet. The bloodied Ranjit was skidding to a halt beside him, crouching to lay his fingers against his throat to feel for a pulse.

And suddenly, sound exploded back into Cassie's ears. She could hear Jake's moan of pain, Isabella's desperate quest for reassurance that everyone was OK, Ranjit's insistent repetition of Richard's name . . .

Reflexively Cassie put her hands over her ears, but then shook herself and ran over to help Ranjit. As she fell to her knees at Richard's side, she felt something sticky beneath her on the floor. Blood, she thought with a creeping sense of dread. *A lot* of it . . .

'Richard?' she croaked.

Ranjit put a hand on her shoulder without a word, and she felt her stomach plummet. Wildly Cassie looked up at him.

'The Eldest has gone,' he growled fiercely. 'Damn it. But all she can do is run for now. We need to go after her.'

'Ranjit, we can't, Richard is—'

'Cassie, she's got to be stopped before she consumes more spirits, gets even stronger. We've got to go *now*.' He paused and gave Richard a last pitying look, and his voice softened. 'Or I'll go for now. Follow me when you can.' After giving Cassie's shoulder a quick squeeze, he raced out of the cave.

Isabella came over and stood above her, propping up Jake, who still looked dazed and semi-conscious. 'Marat's gone too,' she said, her voice laced with anger and shock.

Just for the moment, Cassie didn't care. She could only stare down at Richard, stroking his hair. His face was grey, the veins at his temples purple and prominent, and his eyes were wide and scared.

'Richard,' she whispered, stroking his cheekbone.

'Hope this. Makes up for it,' he gasped, a smile trembling on his blue lips.

'Makes up for what – letting me in on all this fun? Wouldn't have missed it for anything.' Her throat dried and her eyes burned.

'Me either. Wouldn't have missed it. Well . . . not sure about this part . . .'

'Shut up a minute.' Cassie lifted the hem of his bloody shirt to see where the Eldest had ripped a chunk like a shark bite from his side with her claws. She felt a shock of horror run through her at the sight of the wound. Quickly and delicately she let it down again, and he gasped with pain. Cassie tried to imagine getting Richard out of the cavern. Down Mount Kenya. Along dust roads to the nearest hospital – and where the hell was that, anyway?

Not a hope in hell.

'Halton-Jones, why did you have to play the hero? You stupid bugger.' A tear rolled down her cheek, and she wiped it fiercely with the back of her hand.

'Play at it is right. And I was hardly an . . . Oscar winner . . .' He broke off, coughing hard, and Cassie's heart quickened at the sight of blood on his lips. She reached down and wiped it away.

'You saved our lives, you crazy loon. But I told you, shut up. Don't waste your breath.'

'Can't expect me to stop talking. Change habit. Of a lifetime.'

'Listen, Richard, I'm going to get help for you and Sir Alric. Don't move.'

'Ha ha.'

Cassie started to get to her feet, but she felt his fingertips scrape her calf desperately.

'Don't leave.' There were tears as well as blood on his face. 'Please.'

She hesitated only for a second, then knelt back down and put a hand on his chest. She could feel his rapid desperate heartbeat, the shallow tortuous rise and fall of his ribcage.

'Richard . . .' she sighed, fighting desperately to keep the tears back.

'Wh-what?'

'I love you.'

His head rolled round to face her, and his lips curved in a smile, his eyes brimming with tears of his own. 'I'm going to tell Singh on you.'

'You do that.' She couldn't stop crying now. 'You tell him as soon as we get back. See where it gets you. He already knows, anyway . . .'

'Well, in that case. I hope he knows. I love you too . . .'

Leaning into him, Cassie placed her hand on his clammy cheek and carefully brought her lips against his. When it didn't seem as if she was going to hurt him, she kissed him gently.

She felt the moment his breath stopped.

Drawing back, she saw the faint white light of his spirit coil from his parted lips, drift with a thin mourning wail towards the roof, then evaporate into the dank air of the cavern.

Richard's eyes were still open, but the mischievous spark was gone; they were dull and dead. Very gently Cassie put her fingertips on his eyelids and drew them down, then pushed herself up. Every bone and muscle in her body was screaming with pain, and her heart was wrung with grief. She let out a deep, strangled sob.

Cassie felt a hand touch hers, but she shook off Isabella's comfort. Tears were streaming down the Argentinean girl's face, and Jake stood staring at Richard, stunned.

'Isabella, stay with Jake and Sir Alric.' Cassie's voice was hollow. 'Look after them. I'm going to help Ranjit.'

'Wait.' Jake was shaken out of his shock, and seized her arm. 'Cassie. Take these.'

Turning impatiently, she stared at his outstretched hand. The last tiny vial of Tears; all that was left of the precious liquid.

'It's too late,' she said bleakly, shaking her head. 'I don't think they'd have helped anyway. He's gone—'

'No, listen. Sir Alric's note, the one he left in his study? It was about these. He thought they could stop the Eldest. If they touch her.'

Cassie stared at him. 'What?'

He opened her palm, pressed the vial into it. 'It said something about the Tears' ancient origins, them being the thing to stop the Eldest. I don't know how. Just use them. I wanted to . . . I wanted to do it myself. I'm sorry.'

She shook her head. 'But what if—'

'Listen, just take them. Do it for me. Me and Jess, OK?'

'You and Jess.' She curled her fist round the vial. 'And Richard.'

'Yes. Now go!'

Grief was kindling into fury inside her, and even the darkness in the cavern was stained red through her vision. Turning deliberately away from Richard's body, she snatched up the Knife in her other hand.

'This is it, Eldest,' she hissed. 'I'm coming to get you.'

CHAPTER TWENTY-TWO

Cassie burst from the cavern entrance into a pale golden Kenya dawn. Between the trees, the horizon was a very distant line, hazy with glowing watercolour tints, but she had no time to admire it. She plunged down the rocks into the valley and ran. If she ran fast enough, she might even outrun the sight of Richard's broken corpse, branded in her mind's eye.

She stumbled, tripped and fell, rolling down a small gully with the breath knocked out of her, but she leaped back to her feet and ran again. She must be close to the lowest slopes; she could hear the sound of the river they'd followed. It wasn't hard to follow the trail: broken branches, scored rock and blood. Gritting her teeth, she hurtled on down, leaping tree roots.

I'll get there. I'm coming, Ranjit . . .

Abruptly she skidded to a halt. The river pooled

between two waterfalls, a broad placid lake that funnelled into a roaring cascade. But it wasn't the water that brought her to a halt, sniffing the wind, straining her ears. Her Few senses bristled.

Was she imagining things? Cassie took another hesitant step towards the clear riverside path, frowning.

Shadows stirred, and a squat, malevolent figure stepped out from behind rocks.

'Marat.' Cassie shook her head. Of course. Trust him to turn up at the worst possible moment.

The little man grinned at her. 'That's far enough, Miss Bell.'

Five words. Was it the most he'd ever spoken to her?

'Not quite far enough,' she spat. 'Get out of my way.'

His pale raisin-eyes were filmed in scarlet. For a moment Cassie was shocked – wasn't Few status supposed to confer beauty? – but she had no time to wonder. Marat crouched, and sprang.

Roaring, she leaped to meet him. They collided in mid-air, and tumbled, snarling and biting, tearing violently at one another. She kicked him away, but he rolled, recovered, and charged like a bull into her midriff, knocking her on to her back. Cassie yelled with frustrated rage. She hadn't regained her full strength yet, and his stocky frame was surprisingly powerful.

Marat had a grip on her neck, and he tried to squeeze harder as she writhed, trying to get free of him. 'You think I'll let you ruin everything now?' he growled. 'I'll be glad to see the back of you, Bell.'

'Not . . . going . . . to happen,' she rasped, choking for breath.

He laughed, an oddly high, ringing sound. 'You're too weak! Like that arrogant bastard Darke. Too weak, in the end!'

That was what he thought. As his grip loosened momentarily, Cassie struck at him with one arm, knocking him backwards.

'My mistress has sacrificed herself to the Eldest,' he shouted angrily, trying to regain his footing. 'You think I'll let that be in vain? And my young mistress is now one with the greatest of all of us! You're not even fit to be struck down by him!'

'You sound like a bad cartoon!' Cassie yelled, kicking out savagely at his groin, but he grunted, catching her leg, gripping and twisting. Cassie lashed a fist into the side of his face, loosening his hold enough to let her free herself from his grip, but she slipped, knocking into Marat and sending both of them rolling to the edge of the river and into the shallow, murky water.

Marat went for her again, grabbing her head and trying

to force it down under the surface. Cassie struggled, choking, but she managed to twisting a leg round his ankle and unbalance him, sending him splashing into the muddy water. She surged up, sucking in lungfuls of air, coughing hard. As she struggled towards the bank, she felt a grip like a vice close on her ankle, dragging her back. Giving in to the pull, she turned, kicking out, and then, with a roar of frustrated anger, Cassie smashed a fist into Marat's nose. I have to get away from here, she thought, I have to get to Ranjit! Blood spurted from Marat's nose and he cried out in pain.

But he still wouldn't relent. Ugly he might be, but Marat's spirit was clearly not so weak that he wouldn't be able to beat her in her present state. Cassie was already exhausted. A foot connected with her gut and she doubled over, then a hand smashed into the back of her neck and she was back in the water.

You might have warned me, Sir bloody Alric . . .

Cassie blinked, desperately holding her breath. She could see almost nothing in the shallow water at the edge of the river, especially now that they'd churned up the mud with their battle. Strands of weed tangled round her legs and in her hair, and shadows started to pass across her vision. Long, sleek, swift shadows. She was going to drown.

No.

Twisting violently, she finally got away, rolling over and seizing Marat by his thick throat. Snarling, spitting mouthfuls of vile muddy water, Cassie snapped her head forward, felt her skull connect hard with the bridge of his already-broken nose. Marat gave another scream of pain and rage, stumbling back, and Cassie scrambled for the bank. Get out of the water get out of the water . . .

She spun round as soon as she was on semi-solid ground, sliding and skidding in the mud, but keeping her footing. Marat, shoulders hunched, blood streaming from his face, was staggering towards her again, his red eyes brilliant with killing-fury. Curling her lip, sucking in air, Cassie remembered something at last.

Fumbling at her belt, she reached down and gripped the hilt of the Knife.

She drew it and held it out before her. Marat's eyes turned to slits of spiteful malice. Ankle-deep at the river's edge he paused, tilting his head as if to guess at her next move. If he gets this Knife off me, I'm dust, Cassie thought, gripping it tighter.

That thought must have occurred to Marat at exactly the same moment. His lips stretched in a vicious grin, and he wiped blood off his face with the back of a balled fist. He was within an instant of lunging for the Knife when his grin became a grimace, and he let out a sudden short scream. Cassie backed away, startled. For an insane moment she thought he'd stumbled on a log in the water.

But it wasn't a log.

Marat fell forward on to his face, clutching at handfuls of thick mud, and Cassie saw his leg. Incredulously, she realised it was gripped in a crocodile's jaws. The creature was pulling him back now, and he could get no hold on the soft riverbank.

The sight was horrendous. Somewhere in her brain, an automatic humanity switched on. Plunging forward, Cassie grabbed at his reaching arm and hauled on it, but it was too late. The jaws snapped once, taking a better grip of Marat's thigh, and a moment later the crocodile was dragging him relentlessly out into the water. Cassie could see other shapes now, cutting silently through the water to where blood was pooling on the grey-green surface of the water, while Marat thrashed and screamed.

Cassie stumbled back, staring in horror. As the creature moved into the deeper water, Marat twisted, belatedly, hammering uselessly at its eyes and head, striking it with his fists. The crocodile shook its great prehistoric head, thrashing him twice on the surface with a sound like beaten laundry, and then began to submerge.

Cassie could no longer see the creature, but she saw

Marat's face, turned once more towards her, beseeching. As his mouth and nose went under the water his screams stopped, and his terrified eyes were the last thing she saw of him.

And then there was nothing but a spreading pool of blood, staining the thick water a dark and hideous muddy red.

CHAPTER TWENTY-THREE

Panting for breath, Cassie ran backwards so fast she stumbled and fell on a rock, but then she was up and running towards the thinning trees. The Knife was still in her hand and she kept it there, clutched tightly.

No, she thought, no. Not back to the trees. Downhill, downhill. Go back to the river path, you'll get to Ranjit faster.

Her lungs ached and stung, but she stumbled on down the uneven slope, meeting the thin beaten path at an angle. The roaring in her ears could have been her own blood or the river rapids, she didn't know. Where was Ranjit? Where was the Eldest? The fight with Marat had held her up far too long. She was further behind than ever. Tripping on another tree root, she fell hard on to her face, scraping blood from her palms.

Goddammit, Estelle. You said we could do anything

together! Now do it!

No more disembodied voice in her head; no more snide remarks. Just a sudden gathering of strength, as if her spirit was concentrating all her reserves. It wasn't Estelle and Cassie any more; there was no separation. She was Cassie Bell – one of the Few.

Just run.

Cassie grabbed a branch and hauled herself to her feet. I won't let Ranjit down. Power surged back into her limbs, and though the pain was still there, it meant nothing. With a low snarl, she sprinted down the hill.

The ground flew beneath her feet; there was no more tripping, no more stumbling. Her body felt like a featherweight as she raced, and her power was electricity in her limbs. Following the trail of wreckage, following the path, she sprinted over a ridge of ground, sprang down into a hollow beside a cliff.

And as she did so, Ranjit collided with the ground at her feet.

Cassie staggered, almost stumbling over him, crying out in surprise. Seeing who it was, she reached down and clasped his hand to haul him up. He gave her the briefest of looks, then they turned together to face the Eldest.

The monstrous creature roared, raising herself to strike again. As the pounding of her own blood calmed in her ears, Cassie recognised the roaring rush of water. Just metres from where they faced the Eldest, the brooding river vanished over an edge into nothingness, hazed with spray. They were on the edge of a huge waterfall.

'Take her from two sides,' gasped Ranjit.

He attacked again. Running to the other side, Cassie launched herself at the Eldest's back, catching and gripping on tight, tearing at the silver-blonde hair of Katerina's shell as she wrenched the monster's head back, desperate to snap the vertebrae. Not a chance. The Eldest's spine rippled nightmarishly like a snake, and Cassie was flung backwards and slammed against a tree trunk. She sprang back instantly, in time to see Ranjit attack the Eldest yet again, lunging his fists into her powerful torso. The Eldest simply grabbed him, swinging him sideways, and he flew through the air and collided with Cassie.

As they scrambled back to their feet, his eyes met hers. 'She's too strong . . .' he gasped.

'We've got to try—' Cassie said desperately, but as she spoke, the Eldest's clawed hand caught her face with a glancing blow. Reeling back, Cassie put a hand to her cheekbone and brought it away dripping blood. She was playing with them, Cassie realised.

'Scarred!' The Eldest screeched at the delicious irony. 'Like my dear Katerina was.'

'Yeah, but I'm not just a pretty face.' Cassie jumped and kicked, catching the Eldest in the ribs, but she might as well have been made of rubber. The Eldest laughed, caught her ankle, and tossed her aside. Spray from the torrent beyond made an incongruous rainbow halo around them as she flexed Katerina's newly-supernatural muscles, smiling.

'You're wasting your *time*,' the Eldest boomed. 'And mine.' Languidly, she flashed a fist into Ranjit's jaw, and he tumbled towards the edge of the cliff. He tried to raise the Pendant again, but the Eldest stalked to him, seized his wrist and wrenched the jade from it with ridiculous ease.

'You . . . fool!' Contemptuously the Eldest brandished the Pendant. The creatures carved into the jade writhed with terrifying energy. Ranjit held up an arm to shield his eyes as a stronger and stronger light glowed in the heart of the jewel.

'I won't soil my hands on you any further,' the Eldest hissed, and a sickly light began to swirl and gather within the jade. 'I'll have that spirit now . . .'

With a shriek Cassie flung herself on to the Eldest's back, but was again knocked with a violent blow to the ground. The Eldest turned to give her a smirk, and held out a hand, the claw-fingers beckoning. 'I'm waiting,

Cassandra. Give me the Knife.'

A vision flashed across Cassie's mind: Richard, torn apart by the Eldest and lying dead in the cavern on the mountain. Her friend. And then her friend Jake, handing her—

On her knees, Cassie bent forward, gasping for breath. Her fingers trembled as she reached into her shirt, and the Eldest gave a low scornful chuckle.

Cassie raised her eyes to the poison-green glow of her adversary's.

'You asked for this,' Cassie growled.

The Eldest's green eyes brightened, momentarily, with greedy anticipation.

Then Cassie whipped out the last vial of Tears and threw them hard at the hideous monster.

The shatter of glass echoed even above the noise of the waterfall. A rain of crystal exploded against the Eldest's chest and she reeled backwards, clutching at her ribs in disbelief. As the pieces of broken vial tinkled to the rocky ground, the last of the Tears of the Few trickled down Katerina's former body, hissing and steaming as if they were boiling volcanic spray.

The Eldest screamed, raking her chest with her claws. She recovered her balance at the lip of the cliff, drawing herself up with a howl of unearthly fury. Cassie staggered towards the Eldest, unable to tear her eyes away. She was in agony, and raged with maybe her first experience of real terror from Cassie and Ranjit's onslaught. Her body was curling, twisting, writhing.

But *not* dying.

Cassie shut her eyes, desperate. If the Tears hadn't killed her, there was nothing else for it. She didn't dare glance, one final time, at Ranjit. Gritting her teeth, Cassie simply flew towards the Eldest. She snapped her monstrous head up just a fraction of an instant too late. Cassie cannoned into her, and taken by surprise, the Eldest gave a terrible scream.

Then together they plummeted over the edge of the cliff.

It seemed to happen in very slow motion. Cassie heard Ranjit's shout of despair, but it was too late to worry, too late to think or regret.

The two of them were falling, clasped in a deadly embrace, her and the Eldest, twisting in the air. The Knife was in Cassie's hand; she didn't even have to remember it now. Because the Knife was her hand. The cats and snakes and mythical beings coiled and swarmed over her fingers, her palm, her wrist. It was part of her.

Cassie drew back her hand and the blade, and with

one great jolt, she punched it hard into the ribs of Eldest.

A hideous, unearthly screech filled her ears, drowning the roar of the torrent. It seared her brain, filling it, but only for a lightning-instant.

Then they hit the roaring river below.

Cassie did, at least; the moment the Eldest touched the water, she imploded into dust, vaporised on the air.

Cassie fell through the remnants, through water, and into darkness.

The silence was blissful. Cassie felt the water's current catch her as she drifted down, but there seemed no point in fighting it. She didn't have the energy; stunned by the fall and the impact, by the final struggle, and by her wounds that were draining blood into the water around her, she was out of even spirit-energy.

This is it.

Her hair drifted across her face, and she opened her eyes and saw deepening green shadows. There was time to think, and to hope she'd drown soon . . . that it wouldn't take too long . . .

But I did it, she remembered. I did it. The Eldest is dead. And Isabella and Ranjit and Jake are alive . . .

Oh but I wish . . .

Her own thoughts. No Estelle whispering inside her

head, not any more. They were one, sinking into darkness together, down and down. At least she'd made the spirit happy at last …

Ranjit . . . I loved you . . .

I can't fight any more.

I'm sorry.

There was still light, right above her. Gazing up to look at the last of it as she sank, Cassie saw a dark shape, and the pale wash of the sun rippled out in rings.

The light broadened, the rings widened. At its centre, the sunlight was stronger. Real light, not the otherworldly Few light she'd seen all too of much in that last ordeal. Good that it would be the last thing she saw. Cassie closed her eyes, smiling, and opened them again as the last bubbles of air trickled from her nose.

Parting her lips, Cassie started to take her last breath, taking in the cool, dark water—

And arms went round her. A powerful grip dragging her up and away from her death.

Ranjit!

But I'm dying. I'm dead.

Anyway, he loves me. He's holding me while I die. He loves me . . .

Together, they exploded from the water.

Cassie gave a great gasp as Ranjit let her drop to the muddy bank. Air flooded her lungs in a great rush, and she rolled on to her side, coughing violently, choking and spitting. The Knife was still clutched in her palm as if soldered to her hand, but as she clawed at the mud, it unravelled itself from her flesh and she dropped it. Ranjit was holding her shoulders, hammering the flat of his hand into her back, and she vomited river water. She groaned, and he pulled her up and into his arms, gripping her head and cradling it against him, then kissing her face.

God, she thought. I'm covered in stinking mud and we're both soaking and I just threw up what felt like the bloody Limpopo. He shouldn't be kissing me . . .

She kissed him back, wrapping her arms round him, weeping helplessly. What the hell: she was wet already. And so was he.

'Cassie, for God's sake. That was insane. Oh God, Cassie, you're alive. I love you . . .'

Warmth spread through her chilled body and darkness crept across her brain.

And then she blacked out.

CHAPTER TWENTY-FOUR

A light breeze rippled through the kikuyu grass, smelling of dust and hot sunshine. Invisible in the bright-red flamboyant trees, birds fluted and sang, and a troop of vervet monkeys racketed through the branches, then paused, curious, to watch the mourners below.

Cassie closed her eyes and breathed the scents, glad the memorial service was over. She was glad to have Ranjit on one side, Isabella on the other; it felt as though they were propping her up.

The three of them and Jake drew away from the dispersing crowd as Cassie glanced back at Sir Alric, in quiet conversation with Richard's parents.

'That was beautiful,' she murmured, 'but . . . bloody awful.'

'Darke's eulogy was pretty good.' Jake sounded as if he was clutching at straws.

'I barely recognised Richard in it.' Cassie's low laughter was shaky. 'I don't think he would've, either.'

Ranjit squeezed her hand gently. 'We should go and speak to his parents.'

'I know,' said Cassie bleakly.

Isabella put an arm round her waist. 'No hurry, Cassie. They're surrounded at the moment.'

'Poor Perry,' said Cassie, nodding at the American boy. He was openly in floods of tears, consoled by the ever-dependable Ayeesha and a slightly embarrassed Cormac. Some of the other Few had already hurried away – Sara and her gang among them – but others were chatting desultorily, reluctant to go back to the Academy building, waiting their turn to speak to the Halton-Joneses. Cassie was surprised and somewhat consoled by the grief shown by so many of the students, Few and non-Few. Maybe Richard, for all his easy charm, had never really known how well liked he was. She wiped her hand across her cheeks, feeling them wet with tears all over again, and Ranjit kissed the side of her head.

'I'm still amazed he had it in him,' said Jake quietly. 'Who'd have thought?'

'Me,' said Cassie. 'I knew it.'

'So did I,' said Isabella.

'I—' Ranjit swallowed. 'I didn't. I wish I had. He was

there for Cassie when I wasn't.'

Coming to a halt, Cassie turned to him and pulled his face down for a kiss. 'Don't be daft,' she said softly.

'But it's true.' He returned her kiss. 'And I'm sorry. It won't happen again. Ever.'

She knew it. She didn't think she'd ever been more certain of anything. He hadn't left her side since she'd regained consciousness in her own room at the Academy, and she had it on Isabella's authority that he hadn't left her side before then, either. Cassie was still hazy on the details of how they'd got her down from the mountain, rescued Isabella and Sir Alric and recovered Richard's body. But the details could wait. Of Katerina and Brigitte, of course, there had been no trace but dust. There had been remnants of Marat, but only that: remains. A piece here, a piece there. Cassie shivered at the thought, remembering his face as he was dragged under . . .

And if it hadn't been for Richard, it could have been *them* who were dust, and the Eldest would be free to ravage a whole world.

'I can't put it off any longer,' she murmured. 'I'm going to speak to Richard's parents.'

'I'm right with you.' Ranjit hugged her.

She smiled. 'I know.'

* * *

Sir Alric was still walking with a limp. Cassie noticed that, and the remaining bruises on his handsome face, as she shook Richard's father's hand and withdrew, letting Isabella take over with her own achingly difficult words of sympathy. The headmaster was clearly planning to intercept the four of them when they had spoken to the Halton-Joneses, and Cassie didn't have the will or the energy to avoid him. Anyway, she'd barely had a chance to talk to him since the events on Mount Kenya. And there was a hell of a lot to discuss.

Halting in front of them, Sir Alric studied them soberly. 'Cassie. Ranjit.' He turned to the others. 'Isabella and Jake. I'd like you to come to my study, please.'

'Now?' said Isabella, surprised.

He gave a shrug of his elegant shoulders. 'I can't think of a better time. Our conversation is overdue, don't you think?'

With a glance at Cassie for confirmation, Ranjit nodded. 'No sense leaving it any longer.'

Cassie gazed around the study shelves. It was as if nothing had changed since the day she'd arrived this term. It had barely changed since Paris, she thought, as the low table caught her eye. She was even sitting in the very same chair: the one she'd sat in as Estelle Azzedine assessed her, not as a student, as Cassie had thought at the time, but as a host.

Even Sir Alric's world must have been rocked to its foundations by the recent events, but his study remained an unchanging point of stable certainty. It made her smile, ruefully. The books were lined neatly on the shelves; the lamp shone unbroken on the desk. The only object that had been moved was the Urn, which now stood on the desk, the Knife and Pendant laid beside it. The carvings on all three were opaque, glowing only in the normal dappled sunlight streaming through the window, and the creatures were still and unmoving. Cassie's hand twitched as she recalled how they had twined round it, binding themselves to her, aiming her strike at the heart of the Eldest in Katerina's body.

'What's going to happen to them now?' asked Jake. 'The artefacts?'

'Ah. The Council are aware that the Urn survived; that much I had to tell them, for reasons we will discuss. It will be taken back into the Council's care.'

'And the Knife? And the Pendant?'

'Why, Cassie. You were there. You know they were lost in the deepest of Mount Kenya's rivers.' His face remained impassive.

Cassie shook her head, gazing at the three artefacts.

'Sir Alric . . . why? Why haven't you told them?'

'Why do you think? You know how dangerous these are. I'd rather they were kept well apart, and I'd rather the Knife and the Pendant were considered lost forever. The Urn has little use without them.'

Cassie nodded slowly. 'That makes sense.'

Sir Alric touched the Urn gently with a forefinger, then resumed pacing behind his desk. 'It's odd,' he mused, 'but I still miss Marat.'

'That *is* bloody odd,' remarked Cassie, with a lift of her eyebrows.

He gave a low laugh. 'He was at my side for a long time. Playing a long game, no doubt,' he said sorrowfully. 'But I came to rely on him. Foolishly. Of course, it was Marat who broke in here at the beginning of term, trying to get the artefacts. I should have known it, but I didn't want to think it could be true. I was trusting – an all-too-human trait.'

Ranjit and Cassie, sitting close together, exchanged glances. It was Ranjit who coughed and said at last, 'If he was with you for so long, what on earth was his motive for doing what he did?'

'Ah.' Sir Alric glanced at Jake, not quite meeting his eyes. 'A similar story to Jake's, I fear. An out-of-control Few student, Marat's cousin, and death by feeding. Marat

265

chose to take his revenge in a far slower and less obvious way, however.' He winked solemnly at Jake. 'Marat was already Few, but with a very weak spirit. He came to me, requested a job at the Academy. His spirit had never been especially ambitious in previous incarnations, and neither was he. I felt sorry for him. What else could I do?'

'Offer a member of his family a place at the Academy, like you did after Jess died?' observed Jake acerbically.

'Ah. It was Marat who convinced me that offering you a place could do no harm, only good. He did make reference to himself, and to his own situation.'

'In that case,' Jake tightened his fingers round Isabella's, 'I've got at least one thing to thank him for. Sort of.'

Sir Alric nodded. 'I suppose so, though his motives were never honourable. I'm afraid I had rather a blind spot where he was concerned.'

'Full blinkers,' muttered Cassie, not quite under her breath.

Isabella, never one to encourage a scene unless she'd instigated it, clapped her hands and leaned forward, interrupting. 'But what about the Eldest? Katerina's obviously finished, but is he? For sure?'

'Oh, yes. He'd joined with her; they were one. When she died, he died.'

'And you're sure he couldn't survive in another form.'

Sir Alric gave a light shrug. 'It's never happened before. Ever. Yusuf, Mikhail, Keiko – their spirits all died with them. A spirit cannot live without a host. Why would the Eldest?'

In the silence Cassie and Sir Alric turned to look at the Urn, placed so innocently between Knife and Pendant.

He heaved a sigh. 'Cassie . . . I know Estelle is fully inside you now. Has that changed nothing?'

'It's changed everything, and nothing. I know what it's like now. I know what it means. Even more than I did that time in New York, when I managed to throw her out again.' Cassie closed her eyes briefly, recalling when once before in desperation she'd allowed Estelle to fully inhabit her. It felt odd, sitting here discussing the spirit's fate without the old bat's caustic interjections. Cassie almost missed her nagging voice. Almost.

Sir Alric stared out of his window. 'So the one thing that hasn't changed, Cassie, is your mind.'

'Yup.'

He sat down behind his desk and rubbed his eyes. 'I'm sorry.'

Cassie started to get to her feet, though she didn't let go of Ranjit's hand. 'We had a deal!'

Sir Alric sat back and steepled his hands in that thoughtful pose she knew so well. 'We had a deal – not that you kept your side of it terribly well.'

'You can't do this! You can't refuse me!'

'Calm down, Cassie. I didn't say I'd renege on our deal. I said I was sorry. And I am sorry. Sorry you can't live with Estelle, and that you won't let her live with you, become you. I think you're ideally matched in so many ways.' He crooked a smile. 'And the old bat was a surprisingly good friend of mine.'

Slowly Cassie sat back down. 'So you'll let me use the artefacts?'

'If I can't talk you out of it. But I have to try.'

Cassie took a deep breath. It wasn't as if she didn't understand. 'I don't want to hurt Estelle. I sort of like her, actually. But I don't want her to be part of me, and I don't want to be part of her. I didn't want any of this, you know that. And another thing. The most important thing, but if you say it again, I'll feel like shooting you: I can't be with Ranjit if Estelle is inside me.'

Ranjit was very still as Sir Alric studied them both, flicking his pen from finger to finger. Cassie held her breath.

'And it doesn't bother you that your . . . status . . . will be different to his? That Ranjit will be Few, and you won't? Think hard, Cassie. Think of what you'll be giving up for an uncertain future.'

'It isn't uncertain,' broke in Ranjit quietly.

Cassie shook her head. 'I appreciate what you're doing, Sir Alric, and I understand. Honestly I do. But I felt it. I felt that power in the cavern, when I needed her help to break away from the Eldest's power. I felt it on the mountain, fighting Marat. I know I needed her then, but I don't want that kind of power forever. That malevolence, Sir Alric, it's not human. It's got nothing to do with humanity.' She bit her lip. 'Sorry if that's an insult, by the way.'

Sir Alric laughed drily. 'If it is, it's one I don't mind. And nor, I'm sure, does Ranjit.'

Ranjit stirred and coughed. 'Sir Alric . . .'

'Yes?' Frowning, Sir Alric turned to him.

'There's something I have to say. I . . .' Ranjit's voice dried, and he glanced at Cassie, squeezing her hand.

'Out with it,' Sir Alric encouraged.

'There's . . . Look, I need to do something. Something . . . important.'

Impatiently Sir Alric raked a hand through his hair. 'Why do I have the feeling I'm not going to like this?'

'Because you won't.' Ranjit bit his lip, then looked at Cassie. 'Sir Alric? I want you to use the Pendant and the Knife on me too.'

'What?'

269

'Draw out my spirit.' Ranjit swallowed hard. 'Free it from me and put it in the Urn with Cassie's. I want to stop being Few.'

Never, thought Cassie, had she seen Sir Alric look so utterly stupefied. The headmaster stiffened, then shoved his chair back and stood up.

'Ranjit Singh? Give up your Few status? Young man, you are the most powerful spirit in the Academy, and you're destined to be one of the most powerful in the Few. Are you out of your mind?'

'Yes.' Ranjit gave Cassie a fleeting wink, then turned back to Sir Alric. 'I've been out of my mind since my initiation. I want to get back into it.'

'Ranjit.' There was infinite sadness in the headmaster's voice. 'You know that's not true. You're like us all: more yourself than ever.'

'I don't want to be more myself. I want to be the self I used to be. And I want to be that person with Cassie.'

Cassie put her hands to her eyes. They were hot and wet, and she realised with shock that she was crying. Glancing at Isabella, she saw that her roommate was, too. Jake was simply looking at Ranjit with an expression of conflicted awe and incredulity and relief.

'You're right, Sir Alric,' Ranjit went on, standing up and drawing Cassie to her feet after him. 'There would be

270

problems if I was Few and Cassie wasn't. I don't know what kind, but I accept there would be. So why bother? I'll be what she is. Human.'

Cassie wrapped her arms round his neck and buried her face in his shoulder. It wasn't just blind, irresistible love, she thought; it was the fact that if she didn't hang on to him, she was going to faint with joy.

Sir Alric didn't speak for a long time. Stretching out a hand, he toyed with the chain of the Pendant, then lifted it up and let it swing, gleaming in the golden light.

'I don't want this,' he murmured. 'I don't want to do this to you or to your spirits.'

'But we want it,' said Cassie. She brought Ranjit's hand impulsively to her lips and kissed it, barely able to believe her happiness. 'We both do.'

Sir Alric rubbed his face with both hands. 'If it's to be done, it must be done now. The Council representatives are flying out this evening to take the Urn.'

'You'll have to explain why there are spirits in it, I take it?' Ranjit sounded curious, but not anxious.

'That I can blame on the Eldest somehow. He took the spirits for feeding.'

'Packed lunch,' muttered Cassie.

Sir Alric very nearly cracked a smile, but didn't succeed. 'And the Council won't be interested in why the human hosts survived, or even if they did.' Very thoughtfully he replaced the Pendant on the desk, then stroked the hilt of the Knife.

'I believe you'll miss this, Cassie.' He tilted an eyebrow.

'Yes,' she agreed, gazing at it. 'But honestly? Not that much.'

Sir Alric clenched his fists and shut his eyes briefly, agitation barely suppressed. 'If your minds are made up – and I can tell that they are – there's no point delaying. Release him, Cassie.' He added drily, 'If you can, that is.'

Very, very reluctantly, Cassie drew away from Ranjit. He gave her hand a last squeeze as they parted; then they both turned to Sir Alric.

'What,' said Cassie, 'no hoods? No chains? No stone altars?'

'All that rigmarole?' Sir Alric shook his head. 'All the rituals are perfectly simple, really. It's just that the Few have always liked our little piece of theatre.' He smiled fractionally, then, his face serious once more, he raised the Pendant in one hand, Knife in the other.

Jake pulled Isabella back a little, in a protective reflex, but as the Pendant started to glow, its energy was all focused on Cassie and Ranjit. Cassie felt nothing at first; then there was a tremendous jolt in her chest, the tug of

272

something pulling away from her. For a horrible moment, it felt like her heart.

Her back arched with the drag of the Pendant's power and she gasped, but no sound came from her open mouth. Dimly she was aware that Ranjit, too, was bending like a bow under the irresistible power of the Pendant. From the corner of her reddening vision she saw his head jerk back, his mouth wide, and then she couldn't see him any longer because her own head was bent back so far, and she was howling silently at the ceiling.

A short scream from Isabella seemed to come from a long way away, but there was no way of reassuring her. Spirit-power was flowing from Cassie's mouth and from her chest, mingling in a stream that flowed towards the Urn.

It was agony. He hadn't told her this part.

Something flashed through the air between her and Sir Alric; something she knew as well as she knew her own hand, something she was never going to see again. Blurred creatures writhed at the edge of her vision. It was the Knife, severing the connections . . .

And then, abruptly, the pain was gone, and so was her connection to the liquid white light. Her head snapped forward again at the same moment as Ranjit's, and they both cried out involuntarily.

Sir Alric held the Knife loose at his side, his hand trembling. The link between them and their spirits was finally broken. Cassie saw blurrily that the jade carvings on the Urn were alive, coiling and rising and falling, writhing in something very like ecstasy as the light poured in from the Pendant that Sir Alric still held above it.

The headmaster wasn't looking at the Urn, and nor was he watching either Ranjit or Cassie. His gaze was fixed on the streaming spirits. They weren't wispy, like the remains of Estelle's had been after Cassie's aborted ceremony. There was a thick twisting rope of glowing light, almost too intense to look at, flowing into the Urn – their two spirits coiled and united. Ranjit was staring too at the brilliant cord of spirit-light, and his eyes were no longer red.

The line writhed, thickened, brightened with a core of lightning. Then it was sucked into the Urn, making it burst into brief blazing light.

And then, it was gone.

They stood, all of them, staring at the Urn. There was still a point of light visible through the translucent jade: a clear brilliant heart like a single star. It was very, very slow to fade. Isabella stepped forward, unable to tear her eyes from the spectacle, and Jake, of course, followed.

Gently Sir Alric touched the Urn, and the light faded. Cassie became aware that even the birdsong and the chatter of monkeys had been silenced; now they started up again as if they had to make up for the pause. A gecko scuttled for cover behind a grinning Maasai mask. A breeze blew through the window, making Cassie shiver and rub her arms.

'I'll be damned,' whispered Ranjit.

'Not any more,' remarked Jake drily.

'What *was* that?' Isabella's voice was hoarse, and she rubbed her eyes – not only, Cassie decided, because she couldn't believe them.

'They fused.' Sir Alric looked as stunned as they were. 'Did you see that? Of course, of course you did. Good lord, their spirits fused.'

Ranjit reached out a trembling hand to touch the smooth carvings of the Urn, so very still and silent now. 'How?'

Cassie barked a sudden laugh. 'They've beaten you. Beaten us all!'

Sir Alric shook his head, but he didn't look angry, only mystified and a little awestruck. 'Yes, they have. They won't be separated again.'

'But they can hardly go to war, either,' said Cassie.

'Indeed. That's going to be one very powerful spirit.'

Ranjit drew his hand away from the Urn, with a single regretful smile. 'Bye,' he told it softly.

'Have fun, you old bat,' whispered Cassie, as tears stung her eyes again. 'You'd better be careful who hosts this one, Sir Alric.'

'Oh, I will. The Council and I will make sure of that. I don't care how long it has to wait; it'll get someone who can cope with it. Someone who won't misuse it, either. And now.' He turned back to Ranjit and Cassie with a thunderous scowl.

Cassie flinched slightly. 'What?' they said together.

'For heaven's sake.' Sir Alric sounded more irritated than ever, but as if he was simply fighting his own instincts, beating down his own regrets. 'Go on. You'd better kiss the human.' He added, grumblingly: 'Both of you.'

Cassie had never been so happy to do as she was told. She felt Ranjit's arms go around her, and she was already reaching for him. Their lips met, and the spark of energy and heat that raced through her veins was nothing supernatural.

All human, she thought, blissful in his arms. All human.

EPILOGUE

Cassie and Ranjit were silent as they strolled along the beach watching the sky deepen to an apricot twilight. Egrets were flying to their roost in the mangroves, beach vendors gathering up their soapstone wares, handlers leading tired camels home. Normal, Cassie thought. Normal life in Kenya. I wonder what normal life was in Paris, in New York, in Istanbul . . . Well. Maybe one of these days they'd go there, and finally find out.

'So,' she asked Ranjit at last. 'You still actually fancy me? I'm not so *gorgeous* as I was.'

He grinned, and pulled her closer against him. 'I fancied you before you were Few, remember? You're gorgeous enough for me.'

'Know what? You'll do, as well.' She came to a stop and kissed him yet again, fingers threading into his silky hair, drawing him so close she felt as if they might melt into one, like their spirits had. 'Thank you,' she whispered into his ear. 'Thanks for what you did. Losing your spirit. I never expected that.'

He gave a light shrug, and kissed her again. 'I lost my spirit and I gained you. It wasn't a contest.'

They kissed again, and Cassie wished it would never end . . .

'Get a room, you two!'

The yell from along the beach made them jump apart with surprise. Ranjit's face broke into a grin and he waved at the figures coming towards them. Cassie laughed.

'Look who's talking,' called Ranjit.

The bantering words unexpectedly sent a shard of grief through Cassie's chest. They reminded her of . . . A shadow crossed her face as the other two strode up to them, swinging their linked hands.

'I miss him. I wish he was here,' Cassie said.

Ranjit didn't even ask who she meant. 'I know,' he said softly.

'Yup. Here we are, the Four Musketeers.' Jake and Isabella had reached them, and Jake touched Cassie's arm gently. 'And strictly speaking, we should have been five.'

'We'd have been none at all, if Richard hadn't been there.' Isabella took Ranjit's hand and smiled. 'Let's just think of it that way. Always.'

Together, the four of them walked further north on the sand.

'Better watch out for muggers and lions.' Jake nudged Cassie. 'We haven't got special protection any more.'

'True.' She laughed. 'And get this! I have a spot!' She pointed proudly at her chin.

'Poor human!' giggled Isabella.

Jake was first to grow sober again. 'What you two did? Leaving your spirits? It was brave. And right. And . . . thanks.' He blushed.

'Least we could do,' muttered Ranjit, staring out to sea. 'Especially me.'

Jake came to a halt in the sand, seizing Ranjit's arm and forcing him to stop too. 'It wasn't you, OK? I know that now. You didn't kill Jessica. And you didn't even try to kill me. That wasn't really you either.'

'Thanks,' murmured Ranjit. 'But it was, a little bit. With you, I mean, not Jess.' He gave Jake a wry grin. 'But really, thanks. That means a lot.'

'We've got something to tell you two.' Isabella's expression had suddenly grown serious, and she clasped Jake's hand tightly. Both of them had an anxious look, and neither seemed willing to say the next words.

Cassie would have to do it. So she nodded, pushing her hair out of her eyes. 'Yeah, we know. You guys are leaving the Academy.'

Isabella's eyes widened, and she cast a mildly suspicious glance at Jake. 'Cassie! We've only just been to see Sir Alric. How'd you know?'

'Nobody told me.' Cassie tapped her temple. 'Residual Few powers. OK, OK, I'm joking! We guessed, all right?' She gave Isabella a hug. 'There wasn't much chance of you staying, after all this.'

'We need to live a normal life for a while.' Jake put an arm round his girlfriend.

'I know,' said Ranjit. 'Makes it easier for us to tell you, anyway . . .'

Jake raised an eyebrow. 'Oh, yeah?'

Ranjit gave Cassie a conspiratorial grin. 'We're leaving too.'

'No!' exclaimed Isabella in surprise.

'Yep. You think I could go back next term anyway? Get bossed around by the Few, and have Sara throwing her weight around? I think not.' Mock-horrified, Ranjit winked. 'And it's like you say. We need some normal life too. I'll find somewhere to finish my studies, and Cassie will too. Whatever we do, we'll be doing it together.'

'And wherever you go,' warned Isabella, with a dangerous look in her eye, 'you'll stay in touch.'

'We wouldn't dare not!' Cassie laughed, and spun her friend round to walk back towards the Academy.

'I for one value my ribs.' Ranjit grinned at Jake.

'And the spirits – or *spirit* – in the Urn? What's going to happen to that?'

'I bet you Sir Alric will persuade the Council to let him have the Urn back. You can't have forgotten what a smooth operator that guy is. And he'll find someone strong and good-hearted to take that pair on, you can be sure of it.' Ranjit shook his head. 'He'll get his own way, like he almost always does. Luckily, Sir Alric Darke's way is usually the right way.'

'Not always,' chimed Cassie, thinking of how hard she'd fought to be free of the Few.

Night was falling fast as usual, and the cicadas and frogs were starting to chorus. Cassie sighed. 'I will miss the Academy. It changed my life. For better and worse.'

'Funnily enough,' said Jake, 'so will I.'

'So let's make the most of it,' Isabella grinned. 'Mombasa oysters, anyone?'

'You've got your appetite back!' laughed Cassie. 'I'll race you to the dining room.'

'Equal playing field, for once!'

'Not likely!' Cassie bolted into a sprint, running hard till she was as out of breath as any normal human being.

Behind her she heard the pounding of the others' feet as they raced at her heels. All the same, she made it to the great front doors ahead of them, and reached out her hands as Ranjit deliberately crashed into her and folded her in his arms.

'Come on, then,' he whispered as Jake and Isabella ran giggling inside ahead of them. He held the door for Cassie, and took her hand, kissing her with lingering promise.

'School's out, Cassandra my love. Welcome to the rest of our lives.'

MIST

The last shred of the mist swirled and drew back, and she saw where she was. She was very, very far from home.

Midnight: a mist-haunted wood with a bad reputation. A sweet sixteen party, and thirteen-year-old Nell is trying to keep her sister, spoilt birthday-girl Gwen, out of trouble. No chance. Trouble finds Gwen and drags her through the mist.

Only Nell guesses who's behind the kidnap - the boy she hoped was her friend, the gorgeous but mysterious Evan River.

www.kathrynjames.co.uk
www.hodderchildrens.co.uk

Hodder Children's Books

If you've got a thirst for
fiction, join up now

bookswithbite.co.uk

Packed with sneak peeks, book trailers, exclusive
competitions and downloads, **bookswithbite.co.uk**
is the new place on the web to get your fix of
great fiction.

Sign up to the newsletter at
www.bookswithbite.co.uk
for the latest news on your favourite authors,
to receive exclusive extra content and the
opportunity to enter special
members-only competitions.